Say You Are My Sister

Say You Are My Sister

by

LAUREL STOWE BRADY

HARPERCOLLINS*PUBLISHERS*

Say You Are My Sister

Copyright © 2001 by Laurel Stowe Brady

www.harperchildrens.com

Library of Congress Cataloging-in-Publication Data
Brady, Laurel.
    Say you are my sister / by Laurel Brady.
        p.   cm.
    Summary: In rural Georgia during World War II, twelve-year-old
Ramona Louise determines to do everything to help her beloved older
sister Georgie keep the family together after the death of their parents,
even to keeping a secret which could destroy their close relationship.
    ISBN 0-06-028307-6 — ISBN 0-06-028308-4 (lib. bdg.)
    [1. Sisters—Fiction.   2. Orphans—Fiction.   3. Prejudices—
Fiction.   4. Race relations—Fiction.   5. Country life—Georgia—
Fiction.   6. Georgia—Fiction.]   I. Title.
PZ7.B72937 Sa   2000   99-87018
[Fic]—dc21   CIP
                                                                      AC

Typography by Alison Donalty
3   5   7   9   10   9   6   4   2
❖
First Edition

A C K N O W L E D G M E N T S

First, I must express my deep gratitude to all those teachers who encouraged me to follow my heart, most notably, Mrs. Hinsdale in the fifth grade and Mrs. Sweeney in high school. Without their support, I would never have dared try.

Thanks, too, to my editor, Alix Reid, whose vision was often clearer than my own. And to my agent, Marcia Wernick, for all her help, and for being a friend.

Thanks to my dear friends, Carol Lynch Williams and Laura Torres. I don't know if it was a weird coincidence or God's vast sense of humor that threw us together, but I treasure both of you.

Thanks to Linda Smith, for her words of wisdom, sense of humor, and unfailing positive spirit. You are a rare and special woman and I am blessed to know you.

Thanks to my incomparable cousin Bob Arter, a supremely talented and good man. Your encouragement meant the world to me. You are always in my thoughts.

Thanks to my mom, Nancy Stowe, for loving everything I've written, no matter how primitive or silly.

Most of all, thanks to my family for the sacrifices they make daily, for giving me space and time, and tolerating my absences, both physical and mental.

And to my dear Jim, thanks for everything.

To Jim, with all my love.
And to Hilary, Jill-Marie, Jay, Camary,
Trevor, Beau, Eli, and Aja,
who are all my treasures

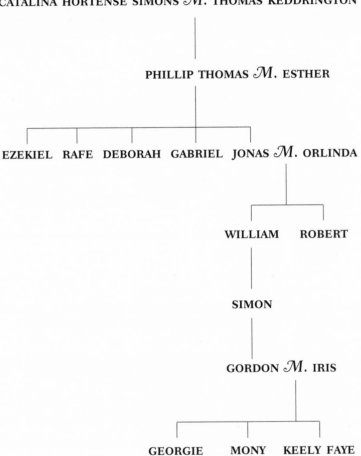

Say You Are My Sister

CHAPTER ONE

It took them three whole days to find my ma. It was Remmy Mack who found her when he stepped on her. Everybody was tired and sick from the looking, Remmy probably most of all, 'cause he was just back from the war minus part of his guts, and his new bride was buried with my ma somewhere under all that mess which was once the church. Remmy was just trying to get a full grip on a busted slab of wall when his foot landed square on Ma. Finding her that way shook him up so he cried and kept saying he was sorry. I wished he'd just shut up.

When Ma kissed me good-bye that April morning, I didn't have no idea she was gonna be dead so quick. I won't never forget my last look at her: pocketbook hanging from her wrist, straw hat trailing the pink ribbon from its bow while Ma marched firmly down the lane toward the trolley. *Onward Christian Soldiers* was all I could think as I watched her. Off she went, forward into battle, going into town to the church where the ladies was having a clothes drive for those poor people in Russia what had been besieged for so long and was nothing but ragged skeletons now.

The day started out real pretty and nice, so the storm took us all by surprise. Pa was out with the chickens, me and my big sister, Georgie, was weeding in the tender new peas. When the wind started howling, it was like some banshee wailing, and all I could think of was soldiers.

Some people don't know what a war is. Us folks in the South know in our bones. This particular war was far away, across the sea in Europe and on a hundred Pacific islands, but every day there was more faces in the paper that wouldn't never be coming home. While we was down there in the pea patch, the war was with us, Georgie and me. We weren't saying it, just thinking it, 'cause it was always right there with us now Georgie's soldier, Private Adam William Carbee, could any minute become dead and gone. So when the wind started howling, all I could think of was soldiers, crying to go home.

Pa, on the other hand, wasn't thinking of soldiers. There ain't been many tornados in Georgia, but he didn't have to see it to know what was coming. He grabbed the baby, Keely Faye, and came tearing through the peas to find me and Georgie, screaming louder than the wind. He yanked us down to the cellar faster than that wind could get us and pushed us all to a corner where we huddled, bent over Keely Faye and holding onto each other. None of us was saying much, and it wouldn'ta done any good anyway, the wind was hollering so. The storm took its time passing us, but when we heard it finally heading off toward Carolina, we peeled ourselves up from the old floorboards to poke our heads outside.

Our farm what had been in my pa's family for most one hundred years was tore up some but spared from the full blast by near a quarter mile. The storm had skipped round, digging out its swath like skipping rocks through town, mashing a house here to matchsticks, leaving one next-door to stand untouched. Our farm was spared, but that don't mean we were the lucky ones.

Just seeing what was left, we knew our ma was gone.

Like I said, it took three days to find our ma squashed underneath the church. Everybody said it was a shame, and I never figured out if they meant a shame she was dead, or that it took the house of God to kill her.

With Ma gone, I couldn't be where Georgie wasn't. Couldn't be alone nowhere. I didn't like to make myself a pest, 'cause Georgie had her own share of grieving for Ma to do. But I couldn't keep myself from following her just like a shadow. Long as she was close, I could stuff the awful hurting far down in my stomach, far enough down so I wouldn't feel it so much.

Me and Georgie, we was half sisters, but you couldn'ta told we was related at all. Georgie's got these big, soft eyes that, once you seen 'em, you could not forget. Dark and mysterious, folks say she is. Like a gypsy or some kind of foreigner. The sight of her thick and curly hair stops boys dead in their tracks. People see us together and they can't puzzle it out, how come she's so pretty and I'm so regular looking. Just straight brown hair, plain old brown eyes, too much nose, and all the rest is knobby knees and elbows. Pa once told me that when I got to be Georgie's age, I'd be just as pretty. Maybe so, but if that's true, God's sure got His work cut out for Him.

In fourth grade Lucy Beckers asked me once if I was jealous of Georgie. Like I was 'sposed to be or something. Jealous? I just stared at Lucy like she was nuts. Even if it wasn't in the Ten Commandments, I couldn't be jealous of Georgie. She was my big sister who loved me fierce and proud, who tightened my braids when they drooped and beat up Charlie Jemissee once for laughing at my spelling test. For years it was just me and her, 'cause Ma couldn't keep babies long enough to get them born. Ma was sick all the time, and Pa was busy with the farm and working at the mill once the war got started. So Georgie was really all I had.

Ma said I should make other friends from town, but it was far to walk just for paying visits and besides, Georgie was the only friend I needed. She could swim and climb and taught me how to hide in hollow trees when we played Civil War and whupped the Yankees. She was smart, smarter than anybody else I knew of 'cept for Pa and Ma. Plus she could sew the fastest, straightest seams of all the girls in school. She won the dress design prize four years in a row, till all the other girls who couldn't draw a bucket of water got mad. Georgie skipped the contest last year to give somebody else a chance. She was like that.

Georgie was so sweet and good that it seemed a wonder she was part of my family. Which made me worry about the day she would not be. Like when she got married.

One night when Ma was still alive, I breathed into the darkness the thing that was so much on my mind. "Georgie," I whispered, "Georgie, are you going to go away?"

She turned over in her bed. The dark was thick, but I could feel her big, dark eyes, looking square at me.

"Go away?" she finally asked.

"With Adam." I was mad at her for making me say it. I didn't want to say the words out loud, didn't want to think that like so many girls who were getting married overnight and sudden-like, that Georgie might go and marry Adam and leave me and Ma and Pa and baby Keely Faye forever.

Georgie sighed but didn't say a thing. It was a real quiet night. Even tucked up under the eaves of our little bedroom like we were, I could hear the wall clock ticking in the parlor. Pa wound it every night. He'd stand up out of his chair in the corner, yawn and stretch, then walk over to the mantel for the key. That was our sign that the day was done. Georgie and me'd put down our books or fancy work, click off the radio, and kiss him and Ma good night. We would go to sleep, lulled by the ticking of the clock and Ma's gentle rocking.

"Are you?" I asked, sitting up and worried now, 'cause Georgie hadn't said a thing.

"Hush, and lay back down," Georgie soothed me, hearing the worry in my voice. That's when she told me her secret, one she'd never told no one before. She sat up in her bed, her eyes all shiny in the dark so I could see them clear across the room.

"The war is going to be over someday," she told me softly, "and when rations are lifted and people can have butter and tires and stockings again, ladies are going to be sick to death of wearing ugly, wartime clothes that are sparing of fabric. They're going to be wild for lovely dresses and hats and gloves."

"What's that got to do with Adam?" I puzzled.

She ignored my interruption. "I'm going to go to New York City, just as soon as I've saved enough money."

"New York!" This was worse than marrying Adam. Adam lived in Georgia, at least.

She didn't let on she even noticed I'd spoke. She was

looking off into the dark like she could see everything she was saying, talking faster and faster as she went, so fast I couldn't hardly keep up.

"I'll get a job in a fancy store, and I'll learn all about high fashions. Then I'm going to Paris to study couture."

I wondered what was the thing she called *co-chure* but didn't get a chance to ask.

"Pretty soon I'll come back here to get you. Together you and me'll open up a fancy store, maybe in Atlanta, where we'll sell ladies' fashions which will be known far and wide as Keddrington's in honor of us. We'll be famous and rich besides, and have a yacht and buy our own private island to entertain queens and rich folks. Ma and Pa and Keely Faye will live next-door and we'll buy them a long and fancy car, shiny white, and once a year we'll drive back to here to torture the townspeople, specially Charlie Jemissee, for not being nicer to us when we was just farm folks, living here on what's left of our great-great-great-grandpa's farm."

I caught on to the one thing that made sense to me in all of this talking. Georgie would come back. She might go away, but she would come back. I settled back on my pillow, nearly satisfied. It was a big secret, but it was hers, and I kept it for her. I kept it for her even when Dr. Carter Fellowes what had fell in love with Georgie himself shamed Adam into joining the army the very next day, and he left, just like that, without no warning. I kept it even though with Adam gone, there was nothing keeping Georgie from leaving for New York any time she wanted.

No, I couldn't be jealous of Georgie, no matter that my pa called her Princess and he only called me Sis, and my ma curled her hair, while she only braided mine. Georgie was my sister and she loved me and she was pretty inside and out. And if God saw fit to take my ma, He also saw fit to leave Georgie, and it weren't so terrible that way.

CHAPTER TWO

Pa cried like a baby over Ma when she died. The fact she was his second wife only made it worse for him. His first wife, Georgie's ma, died up north in Pennsylvania when Georgie was only three days old. When she was gone Pa took the baby and boarded a train back south, back to this house where he had grown up. He raised Georgie to a toddler, and then he found hisself a new wife, who would be my ma, and Keely Faye's.

Now she was gone, too.

The church ladies came to dress Ma, but Pa wouldn't let them. He said he'd do it hisself and he did. Those ladies drew themselves up right shocked at that but let him do it, 'cause there weren't no choice. All they could do was cluck their tongues and pronounce it scandalous. Pa tried to fix Ma's hair, too, but couldn't get it right. Mrs. Holden was bringing in a pie right then, and she shook her head and said his crying was gonna leave big slobbers all over the lovely dress Georgie made for Ma to wear while resting in eternal peace. Georgie had meant to keep the dress for a birthday surprise, but soon as they laid Ma out muddy and torn in the parlor after digging her out of the church, Georgie took herself upstairs to finish the sleeves and neck and hem so we could bury Ma in it instead. Ma looked like an angel, but her hair was a fright till Georgia pried the comb out of Pa's fingers and sent him off to bed. She fixed Ma's hair, then embroidered "I Love You" on a white hanky, which she tucked into Ma's hand. Ma never went anywhere without a hanky, and Georgie was real good with details.

Everybody says there ain't no worse thing in this world than the sound of dirt hitting the top of a coffin. I think everybody's right. Unless it's the sound of your own pa crying.

After Ma died, neighbors came by to help us out with food and chores. It was Dr. Carter Fellowes that came by first of all the folks. It was plain as anything he was only really coming to see Georgie, now the official condolencing was done.

But Georgie wouldn't hardly talk to him, she was so mad because of what he done, driving Adam Carbee off to join the war so far away from her. I didn't talk to him because Georgie wouldn't, and Pa was too tore up with grief to talk at all, so when he got his fill of all that silence from us, the doctor finally left.

Rocking on our porch that night, missing my mama more than I could stand, I thought on Dr. Fellowes and what he'd done. 'Cause anything was better than thinking of Ma.

Dr. Fellowes was still new in town, and on top of that, a Yankee. Weren't much of a bigger sin he could commit than that, but folks, including us I guess, was right grateful to him when he come down last year to take over for Old Doc Wallace, who was the only doctor in Torsten for almost fifty years. The old doc's arthritis drove him to retire after crippling up his hands so bad he wasn't fit for sewing folks' wounds up tight, but he found hisself a replacement, who was Dr. Fellowes, a young man maybe twenty-five or -six. Old Doc Wallace retired and moved to his daughter's house, and Dr. Fellowes fell in love with Georgie.

'Course, he didn't have a prayer. Georgie was full in love with Adam Carbee, and that's all there was to it. She finally got it through to him there weren't any hope.

So Dr. Fellowes took the matter in his own hands. One day Adam was courting Georgie like they was to be married as soon as she said yes; the next day he was gone, just like that, itching to go fight the Germans and the Japanese both. Since Adam wasn't barely old enough and he had never said too much about going to the war before, Georgie was mighty perplexed about why he left and she woulda stayed that way 'cept Harry Johnson at the barbershop started saying it was all the doctor's idea. What was more, the doctor didn't deny it.

Pa was at the barbershop that day the rumor started, but being as how he never repeated gossip, we had to hear the story from the other folks. Georgie and me was washing dishes in the kitchen when Mrs. Hodges and Mrs. Hedgewick come over. Even though Ma had a hundred and a half things to do, she invited them into the parlor and gave them each a glass of sweet tea. She must have forgotten that we could hear every word spoken in the parlor in the kitchen, because she didn't shoo us outside.

"Mr. Hodges," began Mrs. Hodges, acting like she was all prim and proper, "was at the barbershop yesterday and heard Harry Johnson say Dr. Fellowes told Adam he wouldn't be a man unless he was willing to go to war. And then Dr. Fellowes dragged Georgie in it, saying Georgie shouldn't have no part of marrying a fellow who wasn't any kind of man."

Georgie froze up then, stiff as an icicle, and I could see her hands was trembling, no, shaking, with rage.

Mrs. Hedgewick jumped in.

"If you ask me"—which nobody had but Mrs. Hedgewick didn't take no notice of such details as that—"I don't think Dr. Fellowes had Adam's best interest at heart. Any fool could see from the start how that man is pining over your Georgie, though she's so pretty who could ever blame him? I have to wonder if Carter—"

"Dr. Fellowes," Mrs. Hodges corrected.

"If Dr. Fellowes was thinking more of himself than of his country. If he was, it was a mean thing to do, shaming that boy into going off to fight just so the new doctor could take advantage of the situation—"

"Which he himself created—"

"Of Adam's being gone to see if he could capture Georgie's attention."

"Adam is hardly a boy," my ma corrected. "And Dr. Fellowes is too fine a man to be so devious."

"If he's so fine a man, then why isn't he doing his part for the war?" Mrs. Hodges hated it when Ma defended folks instead of upholding every vicious word that got said around her.

"Because he's a doctor, and our need is desperate here. 'They also serve who only stand and wait,'" Ma quoted in his defense. "But really, here we all are, jumping to conclusions. Not one of us here really knows what happened between my Georgie and her Adam except for them, and they're not telling."

Back in the kitchen, I looked at Georgie kind of sideways, pretending I wasn't really peeking at her face. We'd all tried to find out what it was Adam said to her before he left, but she wouldn't say and by the way her face was twisted round in her rage, I could see she surely wasn't going to spill no beans right now. Her lips was slammed tight together and she went at those dishes, scrubbing Ma's teacups so hard she wound up crushing one to bits right there in the suds.

"Look what you done!" I yelped, horrified.

"What *I've* done?" Georgie sputtered, shaking the useless teacup handle. "What about *him*?" Georgie flung the handle in the dishwater and grabbed up a towel. "That awful man! How could he do—"

I tried to remind Georgie it was just gossip. "Adam mighta gone to the war on his own, and you know you can't never trust a word that Harry Johnson says, anyway" was what I told her. But Georgie didn't seem to hear it.

"Dr. Fellowes had no right to interfere. Who does he think he is? Adam can do his own thinking, thank you very much, and so can I. And if Dr. Fellowes thought such interference would improve his cause, he's got another think coming."

When all the ladies finally took their leave, Georgie climbed the stairs to our room. I was shaking out the dish towel when I saw Ma heading out to feed the chickens, a basket dangling from her arm. I hung the towel up to dry and trotted after her.

"You don't believe those ladies, do you, Ma?" I said when I caught up, forgetting I wasn't supposed to have heard the conversation.

But all Ma said was, "I know my Georgie." She held the back gate open for me. "And I don't think there lives a man or boy who would walk away from her just on account of what somebody else said."

The henhouse was set up off the ground, with a ramp leading from the fenced-in chicken yard up inside it. I didn't like stepping through the mucky yard, but I wasn't done with Ma, and that's where she was going so I had no choice. She filled a battered pail with cracked corn from a burlap sack in the corner and I helped her scatter it by handfuls on the ground. With a lot more commotion than was necessary the chickens came flocking to the corn, running over and past each other in a mess of heads and beaks and sharp claws. I always shuddered at this part, thanking my lucky stars I wasn't born a chicken, living all my life in this dirty corner of our farm. I liked the smell of burlap and corn, though, so I took the empty pail from Ma and replaced it in the sack of feed. Before I closed it down I sucked in a lungful of the smell, closing my eyes to feel the flavor of the grain and bag all mixed inside my nose and throat. After tromping among the chicken droppings in the yard, the grain bag smell was clean and cleansing.

With most all the chickens occupied out in the sunshine, I followed Ma inside the little shed where it was dark and close. Coming in from the bright sun outside was like being slapped blind, but Ma didn't slow her steps, just strode over to where some laying hens was sitting on their eggs. Ma reached underneath those birds to take their eggs, warm and brown and fresh.

It was easier to talk inside, with only a couple mellow birds that didn't have no need to interrupt. "Well, Ma," I continued as she carefully placed the warm eggs in the basket slung across her arm, "you've seen how forlorn Dr. Fellowes is since Georgie told him to get lost. Maybe he wanted revenge."

"I hope," Ma said, and I could see her frowning, even in the dark, "that you don't believe your sister just said to that man, 'Get lost.'"

"Well, I don't know the exact words"—I tried not to sound sassy—"but that was the jist."

"Mony, dear little Mony." My ma shook her head and clucked her tongue as she gave the henhouse one last look around. "You need to learn, sooner or later, people do what they need to do. Adam did what he had to do, Georgie did what she had to, and whatever Dr. Fellowes did, he had his reasons too."

She was finished now, and left the henhouse. I trotted after her, down the little ramp and wading through the chickens again on our way back to the house, trying to hear her above the sound of the fowl. "It's all water gone from us," Ma was saying. "Long passed beneath the bridge and not for us to second guess or even really understand. Just let this be a lesson, Mony, for your future. You do what you must and don't worry what the other people think."

Most of Ma's words went right past me, but I took comfort from them all the same. It wasn't any of my problem to fret over, and if Georgie didn't want to talk to Dr. Fellowes ever again, that was fine by me. Ma had a way of making problems go away like that.

I sighed, rocking on the porch. I had thought that thinking on Dr. Fellowes would keep me from missing Ma. It didn't.

In the first couple weeks we didn't have our ma anymore, Pa was like a dead man walking through days when the sun don't rise. He went about his business like a shadow, like somebody sucked all the gumption right out of him along with most of his living parts. He didn't speak, didn't eat, didn't crack his mouth open from the straight, sorrowful line it was petrified into.

I was hurting myself, but it made me mad to see the way Pa was behaving. Like he was abandoning us, too.

I took to almost shouting at him to get a reaction from him—any sign he still cared—until Georgie told me to stop.

"We have to be strong for Pa," she said.

"I can't."

We was up in our room together, Georgie and me.

"Pa's heart is broke, and that's a burden big as the world," my sister said, sitting me gently down on my bed so she could undo my shoes and socks. "Worry over us suffering about Ma could wring the last life out of him. So we have to be strong. For Pa."

From that time on I tried to follow Georgie's lead, corking up my eyes and stuffing all the sobbing clear down inside me where it would be a secret kept from Pa. I was being strong for Pa and for Georgie, too, who was now mourning Ma and missing her Adam, who had not written her any letters from the army. I pushed my tears down so far and deep they only squoze out of me in the night, when Pa would not hear them, earthquake-sized sobs that woulda tore me apart 'cept for Georgie's arms around me.

But it took a visit from Magnolia Hewitt to shake Pa up.

Magnolia Hewitt had many soft, fine little ways, and if you run across her walking down the street with her dainty and virtuous lady steps, you'da thought she was some kind of gentle southern lady.

But she weren't no such thing.

She proved it in good shape that day she came, seventeen days after Ma's passing. We was all in the kitchen, Pa sitting at the table staring at his hands, and Georgie folding up some laundry fresh from the clothesline and keeping an eye on Keely Faye. I was fixing us some oatmeal for our supper. That's all we ate those days. You'd think a girl most thirteen could fix something besides oatmeal, and I probably could 'cept I didn't have much more mind to fix decent food as I did to eat it. Georgie didn't seem to notice, and Pa was sleepwalking around so, I coulda fed him sawdust and he wouldn'ta complained. But it didn't occur to me to be ashamed of the oatmeal, not till Magnolia Hewitt swept up to our kitchen door and caught us at it.

Pa steered Magnolia in the parlor, and even in the kitchen, we could hear the swishing sound of her silk stockings as she settled herself in a chair. If anybody could get silk stockings now, it would be Magnolia.

Her genteel voice floated into the kitchen.

"Mr. Keddrington, may I first convey my deepest and most heartfelt sympathy for your terrible loss. I cannot fathom what the Good Lord had in mind to call upon a man such as yourself to suffer widowerhood twice, and both times with helpless infants to care for. It shakes the very foundations of one's faith, it does, but we mustn't question what we cannot understand."

"Has Magnolia got religion all of a sudden?" I whispered over Keely Faye's head, holding her up to the sink so's Georgie could wash her little fat cheeks and paws before supper.

"She didn't come here to talk about God's mysterious

ways, I know that much. Hold this baby still, Ramony Louise. I don't trust that woman one bit."

"Mr. Keddrington, it pains me to say it, but a wise man like you will have to acknowledge this is not where that precious infant belongs. A baby needs a mother. Oatmeal for supper, my lands. The very idea sends shivers all through me."

"Oatmeal ain't so very awful," I whispered, incensed.

"Shush," whispered Georgie back, straining to hear Pa's response.

"What we choose to eat is none of your affair, Magnolia, and frankly, I'm surprised a lady such as yourself would feel called upon to mention it." Pa could hold his own, even against Magnolia, for all that she was college educated and he had only got through eighth grade.

"I only mention it because it tells me I was right to come here."

"Why *did* she come here?" I hissed at Georgie.

"Trouble," Georgie replied grimly, her eyes narrowing.

Magnolia was speaking again. "Mr. Keddrington, I know you are a capable man when it comes to earning a fine living for your family. To try to be both mother and father to two young girls while continuing to operate this farm is more than commendable. But, Mr. Keddrington, the baby child is different. She needs a mother's love, and I am here to offer my services in that regard."

"Surely she's not volunteering to leave Mr. Hewitt and become Pa's third wife!" I exclaimed, not understanding why my sister's face was suddenly drained of color.

"No," Georgie's lips were moving, but I could hardly hear. "That's not what she is volunteering. Not at all."

Pa didn't get it right away, either. But there weren't no question when it did sink in. There came a loud crash from the parlor. Stunned, we peeked around the doorway. Pa was towering over Magnolia, rage and blackness in his eyes. His chair was upturned as if he'd knocked it over when he exploded to his feet.

"What kind of a man do you think I am, that I would give my child away?" he roared.

It weren't till then it come to me what Magnolia was after. Keely Faye. She was thinking she could take Keely Faye away from us, and we'd think it a favor. I felt stupid, realizing out of the three of us, Georgie had it figured out the quickest. But it made sense. Magnolia had been a missus for ten years and didn't have no children yet.

Magnolia stood up. Pa's rage didn't seem to bother her one bit.

"No one is asking you to *give* anything away," she said smoothly. "I'm a wealthy woman, Mr. Keddrington."

This was true. Everybody knew she was one of the wealthiest in town, married as she was to the president of the bank. "Of course, no amount of money will take the place of that dear baby, but you will have the comfort of knowing you did right for her sake in giving her a proper mother."

"You must think me a fool," Pa answered. He'd wrestled back control of hisself and spoke calmly. "I may be a simple sort, but any half-wit would know you didn't come here just to be noble. I'm downright sorry you ain't been blessed with no offspring. It must be awful to be lonesome for a baby of your own, but not near so awful you can be excused for coming over here, pretending to have our best interests at heart, when all you want is to steal our child."

"I'm only trying to help," Magnolia answered after a second or two.

If a body wasn't listening real close, they would not have heard the bit of desperation that crept in. Almost, for just a second, I could be sorry for Magnolia Hewitt. Almost.

"Be realistic, Mr. Keddrington." I could hear how she was trying to command, not plead. "In my care, you can be assured that child will be cherished and loved. She will enjoy all the benefits of a home and family, instead of a makeshift life, which is all you can offer her. Who's going to care for her while you are off to your job at the mill? Who's going to curl her hair and iron her little pinafores? Surely not your daughters, who will be at school and all caught up in boys and getting married sooner than you think. Don't you—"

Pa cut her off, and I was glad of it.

"That's enough, Mrs. Hewitt. You turn yourself around and march out that front door and don't you never come back here again. I'm man enough I can forget what you've done today, but you'd best never mention it again."

Magnolia's voice dropped down so sudden it was like a rock throwed off a mountain. "Mr. Keddrington," she hissed. "I don't think I need remind you my husband is president of the bank and an important man in town. He can make your lot very difficult if he chooses."

"You can just take your idle threats and get out of my house and off my land," Pa shot back, and his voice did not leave any room to doubt how much he meant it. "I don't aim to worry over what your husband or his bank think they can do to me."

Magnolia drew on her gloves and picked up her purse. We were standing almost all the way in the room by now. Not realizing it, we'd inched further and further in, mesmerized by what was happening. Magnolia saw us then, and particularly her eyes latched onto Keely Faye, who was cooing and gurgling there in Georgie's arms. Magnolia's lips thinned right down and her eyes went cold as a steel post in wintertime. She turned away from us and looked at Pa.

"Well. We'll see about that, Mr. Keddrington. Why don't I just give you a bit of time to reconsider. Let's say two weeks. Look your situation over, good and hard. Because you'd be surprised to see what a bit of money and some influence can bring about." Then she picked up her purse and headed out, her silly heels click clicking cross our floor, leaving all of us behind in silence.

We all stood kind of stunned in our tracks when Magnolia was gone. Pa was the first to recover. He didn't say a word, just strode past us to the kitchen where our pathetic food was all cooled off and clumped in its bowls. Pa scraped out the bowls, then got down on his haunches, pawing through the pan cupboard. His face told us not to interrupt, so Georgie and me gathered up Keely Faye and scampered out of the place.

When Pa called us back in, he'd cooked us up a decent supper: roasted potatoes and pig and tender new greens he brung in from the garden. He'd even made us a rum cake, in spite of it used up most of our sugar ration for the month. Ma had always disapproved of such truck, but Pa just set it in front of us and cut off giant slabs, plopping them down on our plates which were still sopped with gravy. We ate the cake in silence, not hardly taking note of the gravy, seeing as how the cake was so good. I don't know if the cake and roasted potatoes and pig was his way of showing us Magnolia was barking up the wrong tree or just trying to make up for his weeks of moping.

With our plates finally slicked clean, Pa shoved back his chair and reached for his pipe. That was always a signal some important pronouncement was to follow, so Georgie and me straightened up our shoulders, pushed back our own plates to make room for our elbows on the checkered oilcloth, and waited.

"There's gonna be some changes round here," Pa's solemn voice assured us as he thumped tobacco in his pipe. "We all miss Ma, but there ain't much use in us all going straight to seed over what's happened to us. We got us a farm to run, a baby to raise, and two girls what are near to being women to get started with their lives."

And a pa what's wasted down to sunk-in eyes and hollowed-out cheeks was what I wanted to add, but I didn't guess it would be helpful. Besides, all Pa's bustling round the kitchen that evening seemed to indicate he'd decided to snap out of what was ailing him, and if we had Magnolia to thank for that, I wasn't too proud to admit it.

"Now, we all know I can be a passable cook, when I've a mind to." Pa grinned at us. I nodded back, enthusiastic to agree. Pa had learned to cook pretty good while Ma was sick all those times, losing babies.

"Better than just passable, Pa," Georgie noted, wiping Keely Faye's chin with an embroidered kitchen towel.

"But what I'm better at is farming. Your great-great-great-grandpa didn't carve this place out of wilderness just for me to watch it go to rack and ruin. Which it will, if we don't all set about getting this family back on track." He paused, sucking on his pipe.

"So. I been thinkin'."

"So have I," Georgie chimed in quick. Georgie was a great one for making plans. "I think I should take over the house chores, the cooking and cleaning and washing and such, so you can turn your attention back to earning us a living at the mill. Ramona can get up early with you to tend to chores before you go to the mill, and help again when you get home evenings. And she and I will take turns watching Keely Faye."

I tried not to make a face, but if Georgie thought I'd go near to the cow or muck around with the chickens on a regular basis, she had herself another think coming. If there's one thing I don't cotton to, it's crops and cows. I guess that's two things, but either way, cows scare the dickens out of me, even if their eyes is all helpless and soft. And I didn't have no use for our bull, who in particular frightened me worse than a nightmare. Plus crops means days out in the hot sun, picking weeds and fighting bugs and worms and dirt getting under your fingernails. Driving the tractor would be fun, sure as shooting, but Pa maintained I was too young for that.

"Well," said Pa, and a little shadow crossed his brow. "Well, that is one idea to consider. But I want to suggest a different one instead."

I gulped a little, wondering how much worse his plan would be.

"I was at the Widder Baxter's place the other day. She was near to buried under a pile of fabrics, whining as how she can't get no good help and is overrun with work."

Georgie perked right up at that. "She started taking on custom tailor work, in a little back room at her dress shop," she supplied, and didn't neither of us bother asking how she knew. Dresses and sewing was Georgie's territory, and she kept up with goings-on that affected what she cared about.

"Well," Pa went on, nodding at Georgie's contribution. "I asked her, Widder Baxter, could you use some help around this place? Somebody to do the fancy sewing work, so you can concentrate on serving your customers up in the front. She jist looked at me like I was funning with her and said, 'Gordon Keddrington, I was afraid you'd never ask. What I wouldn't give to have your Georgie in my back room!'"

Georgie dropped her eyes toward her lap. I'd seen her going in the widder's store a time or two, and once she was carrying some drawings, kind of hid under her arm. I wondered if she'd been trying to sell the widder on trying out a few of her designs, the likes of which I knew my sister had a drawerful locked away.

Pa didn't notice Georgie's reaction. "She said that, she did, and I said, 'Well, now, I'll see if that could be arranged.'"

It took Georgie a minute to let it sink in. When she looked up, her eyes was shining like big stars on a clear, black night.

"You mean, she'll let me work there?"

"Yep. She said all the other girls in town was all run off to some factory or other, rather be hammering airplanes together than sewing in her back room. Now mind you, she can't pay what a body could make hammering at airplanes, but I sorta got the feeling you wouldn't like a factory much. And it's high time you started choosing a path for yourself. So if you want it, the job is yours."

I couldn't think of anything that would suit Georgie better. Neither could Georgie. She fairly glowed, and I couldn't help but laugh a little at her happiness.

"As for the mill," Pa said, crossing his legs, "I don't see no reason why I got to keep on going there. Truth be told, I'd rather stay here and work this farm. It ain't been worked proper for a couple years, and a body kin tell that without two glances."

"But Pa," I started. He hushed me with a look.

"It means less money, but in the end, I don't see no reason for me to wear myself out making other people rich. We got us this farm, free and clear, and we could live right smart off what it can produce. When the war's over, price controls will be a thing of the past. Agriculture's going to be more important than ever here in the South. We got us a head start with this here place, and in a year or two, we could be as well-off as most anybody and contributing to the good of our country to boot. Besides." Here he paused, looking at Keely Faye who was trying to pinch a last cake crumb off her plate with chubby fingers. "Besides," Pa went on, still staring at her, "if I stay home, I can watch over Keely Faye and she'll be near as well-off as if her ma was living. I can't be no ma to her, but I can be her pa. Ain't no rich woman gonna ever come in here again throwing guilt all over us on account of this here baby. Not while I got breath in my body."

His words settled around us, drawing us together like a string. We was a family again.

"As for Mony." I jumped as Pa resumed his speech. "Soon as school's out, Mony will be in charge of keeping house." He reached across the checkered tablecloth and patted my hand, what was resting beside my plate. I looked up at him and my heart give a little leap. There ain't nobody can show so much love busting out of him like my pa can, just with a look. "You need to learn to cook, Sis, and keep things picked up and the wash done. We'll all do our part, but it will be your main responsibility. Just until you're old enough to know what you want to do with your life and go out and get a job like Georgie here."

"I can cook," I assured Pa, my mind racing. I'd always helped Ma with the meals and the wash, and if everybody did their share, my load was probably the lightest of all. "And I can help with Keely Faye."

"Good." Pa nodded, and I thought it was a little bit funny he'd made us all happy by giving us work and chores to do. It wasn't New York or Paris, but at least Georgie was gonna be sewing clothes and doing what she loved. And Pa figgered I was more than just a kid now, something he never did before. The farm had been in our family since before the War between the States, but since Pa'd been working at the mill, the place *had* kind of gone to seed. It would be good to see the fields green again, the sagging fences propped, and the sad old barn painted and full of feed and baby animals. As for Magnolia, she'd learn quick not to go poking her nose into our business now that we knew where we were aiming.

No more sitting around wishing for things that couldn't be. For a little bit, we could all believe that tornado carved some kind of a future out for us, even if it wasn't nowhere close to a fair trade for taking away our ma.

CHAPTER FOUR

I can't say Pa stopped grieving the night Magnolia came. But the snap that she brung back to him stayed on, and we started living again like we wasn't being suffocated by a choking fog.

One night we was sitting around the fireplace together, all cozy. Pa lit up a couple logs, not much, 'cause it was pretty warm for so late in April, even if it was most pitch black out. Things was shaping up right fine at our house. Pa had already give his notice at the mill and throwed hisself into the farm in a big way, mending fences, plowing up and planting extra fields of melons, even cleaning out the chicken coop. Them chickens was surprised as we were, seeing Pa up to his knees almost in the muck that had been accumulating in the many months the place was so neglected.

Georgie was contented as a little hen, fussing right now with some handwork on her first big custom project for the widder. Tandy Mick, who weren't no more than eighteen years old, was marrying a gentleman from New Orleans come September, and Georgie was having herself a fine old time with Tandy's ma's dress over in the corner next to Ma's beaded lamp where the light was best. Tandy had got it through her head her ma's dress would have seed pearls tucked into the complicated lacework, and Georgie was having herself a dickens of a time getting it all to lay right. Me, I was enjoying rocking Keely Faye and she was getting right dozy in my lap. Pretty soon I'd take her to her bed, but not just yet.

As I waited for her eyes to close once and for all and stay that way, I watched Pa reading a farm magazine, getting all into a dither 'bout the latest thing in tractors.

"Says here," he throwed out into the quiet, "a body can increase production nearly tenfold with just this one piece of equipment. 'Course, it's better if you can bring yourself to invest in a couple of accessories, like this here disking contraption. And of course, this combine. We could sure have ourselves some fun with that, huh, Mony?"

"Who's this *we*, Pa?" I perked up. I couldn't help myself being just a mite sarcastic. "You got a mouse in your pocket? Last I heard, I weren't near old enough to even consider driving the tractor. You gonna finally break down and let me do it?"

"Hmmph," he said, and I figured that was my answer.

In the quiet we could hear crickets outside chirping, and little peepers off down in the woods. It was nice there, all together like we was. I was curled up around Keely Faye in the rocking chair, her little curls tickling my chin. I had asked Georgie to cut my hair off short for summer, and I mighta looked more boy than girl right then, but I didn't care. Keely Faye knew who I was, and there was plenty of comfort having her all snuggled up against my chest.

The silence in the firelight began to stretch out long. Our radio was broken, blew a tube a couple months ago, and Pa never got around to getting us a new one. It was just as well, I figgered, 'cause the last thing Georgie probably wanted to hear right then was war news.

"Pa," I finally asked, even though it broke the peace and quiet. "Tell us again about our great-great-great-grandpa."

I never tired of hearing about this man. I could just about tell the story myself, how Phillip Thomas Keddrington's ma near got killed by the Indians way back in the beginning of the previous century. But I liked to listen to Pa tell it, 'cause he always added details we hadn't heard before.

"What do you want to hear?" Pa asked, setting aside his magazine, happy for the distraction.

"The whole thing," I said, like I always did.

"Starting where?"

"The Indians," I prompted. Pa knew that. He just always asked because it was part of the ritual we had.

"The Indians." Pa rubbed his chin. "First of all, you have to understand, them Indians was only defending what was theirs. They was only doing what anybody woulda done under the circumstances. So you can't hold it against them."

Pa always told us this, every time.

"We know," Georgie assured Pa, from her needlepoint chair in the corner.

"Well, anyway, Catalina Hortense Simons, that was her name, Phillip's ma, she was just a girl at the time, only a year or so older than Georgie is right now. Her pa built hisself a cabin over there 'bout thirty miles outside Greeneville, Tennessee, where he aimed to settle his family down. He had two big strong sons and Catalina. Now, she was without doubt the prettiest of the lot, but that didn't trouble her none. She grew up with brothers, and a coupla parents who weren't no strangers to working hard to stay alive. They come down here from Baltimore, just after the time of the colonies.

Catalina was the youngest child, just like Keely Faye here."

She musta heard her name, 'cause Keely Faye's eyes slid open lazy-like. I smiled down at her. "Hush, go back to sleep." I said it so quiet, couldn't nobody else hear but her. Her eyes closed again.

"Catalina was born to her pa's second wife after his first died of the cholera. They was in Tennessee only a couple or three years when the Indians acted up. There was lots of isolated Indian troubles, but this time, it was the real thing. Them Indians came across the Simons' cabin one evening, when Catalina was out getting water from the creek. Hearing the commotion, she hid herself in the woods, where she watched her ma get dragged outside and kilt. Her pa took up his rifle, but them Indians kilt him, just like that, then did the same to her two brothers who come running in from where they was tending animals to see what the ruckus was all about. Then they burned the cabin. Catalina was the only one left, and she hid herself two days in those woods, afraid to come out even after them Indians was gone.

"She finally decided it was safe to make her way to the nearest settlement. It was nigh onto thirty miles, mind you, and she didn't have nothing 'cept the clothes on her back, which was tore apart by brambles and branches when she finally stumbled onto white folks."

"You skipped a part, Pa," I protested.

"So I did." He nodded. "Seems once she got started on her way, Catalina run across a couple other burnt-out cabins that the Indians got to first. Everywhere she went, the people was all dead, so she tried to circle round those places, avoiding them because there was nothing there but death. Near neighbors, far neighbors, all gone. All of 'em."

Pa paused, not saying nothing more for a respectable while, thinking of the dead. He took up his pipe and packed tobacco in it, and we waited while he lit it up. Pa didn't really smoke it, more just kind of held it in his hand.

"Pretty soon," Pa commenced to talking again, "Catalina's got herself all lost there in the woods, not recognizing any-place no more, not knowing if she'd ever see a living soul again. She was cold besides, and starving to her core. Didn't have nothing with her 'cept a bucket when them Indians came, and she was near ready to drop, curl up beneath a tree somewhere and close her eyes, never to open them again."

I shivered. I could see as clear as if I was there myself, lost in the forest, alone and cold. Being alone is worse than cold. Worse than hunger, too. Being alone is almost like being dead. I didn't like to think about poor Catalina, hearing forest sounds and scared, with nothing to wrap around her shoul-ders against the night. I clutched my baby sister tighter against me, until she whimpered a little and I loosened up.

Pa's voice went on about Catalina. "She was near to drop-ping when of a sudden, there was a sort of wagon path. Right at her feet, as if an angel dropped her there. So Catalina fol-lowed it, figgering on it coming out someplace, but she kept herself mostly hid in the woods beside the path.

"Her third day walking, she was mighty hungry, as well as tired and scared. It'd been five days now, you know. She's all tore up with brambles, her clothes are shreds, and her stom-ach hurting so from being hollow. She's plumb wore out, ready to give up, just find a tree and close her eyes. When of a sudden, there smack in the middle of the wagon path, she sees a little baby. 'Bout a year or so old, maybe Keely Faye's age. Just laying there, not crying, not nothing, just staring up at the sky, like he was waiting for Catalina to come along and pick him up.

"Well, Catalina, she couldn't no more walk past, leave that baby there, right out in the middle of no place. But she didn't dare go pick him up, neither. She thought it was a trap of some kind, like maybe Indians put that baby there for bait case somebody came along, to get them to stop. So she just sat there, hid, waiting for hours, watching the wagon path, hoping whoever dropped that baby there would miss him and come back to find him. But they never did. There he was, just laying by hisself out in the middle of nowhere, and no explanation why.

"When it started getting dark, the baby kind of fussed a little, taking cold I 'spose. Catalina ventured out of the woods, watching for signs of Indians coming to get her. But there wasn't none. Just her and that baby, which was a little boy, and which she picked up and carried with her, since there wasn't anybody else for miles around to watch over it.

"She carried that baby clear to Greeneville, where she traded her petticoat for a gun and her gold locket for a horse. She took the baby and the gun, and she rode that horse all the way to Marietta, where she thought her pa had friends. She didn't find them, but she met up with a fella there named Thomas Keddrington, who took a shine to her, even if she did have a baby and no husband to account for it, which wasn't considered polite. A scarce month later, Thomas Keddrington married Catalina, and they christened the baby Phillip Thomas Keddrington. That baby grew up in Marietta, became a lawyer, and eventually was your great-great-great-grandpa."

"And that's why we don't know who our ancestors are," I added helpfully.

Pa turned a chilly look on me. "We do so know who our ancestors are. Catalina's people, the Simons of Baltimore who descended from the Pilgrims, and Thomas Keddrington's folks, who came to Marietta direct from Scotland where they trace their lines to royalty. Those are our ancestors."

"But Phillip wasn't really their child."

Pa's eyes narrowed, real stern. Instead of looking at me kindly like was his habit, he glared at me. Even Georgie in the corner frowned, and she wasn't frowning at her thread or needle. She was frowning right at me.

"Catalina and Thomas considered him theirs in every way, and loved him just the same as they loved their other children who would soon come. They considered him a gift from God, just like every child is, and didn't give a second thought to how they came by having him. There's other ways to make a family than simply giving birth to young 'uns. There's more to love than just being there when the seed gets planted."

I felt my face color. Pa, being a farmer, sometimes talked a little too plain for my liking, figuring things like where babies come from, be they people or animals, is second nature and forgetting some folks thought them subjects delicate and grown-up, reserved for only certain times and places.

Pa continued stern-like. "Phillip's parents cherished him, even if they didn't get him in the customary way. Catalina always considered it a miracle she stumbled on him, having just watched her family get hacked to death and needing some good reason to go on. But God puts you where He wants you."

I kind of slunk down in my chair, wishing I could hide behind Keely Faye.

"Phillip's people was their people, never mind who left him in that road," Pa said, like he was just stating a fact, pure and simple.

But his next words was curious, something he hadn't mentioned in the story all the times he told it up to now.

"When Phillip was grown and married, he took in a child hisself, the son from a neighbor farm where all the family took sick and died, leaving that one boy all alone. Phillip raised that boy, named Jonas, like a son, and it was Jonas who was your great-great-grandpa. He was the only one of Phillip Thomas Keddrington's boys who came home from the war. The War between the States, that is."

It made me a little dizzy to discover that another member of my family came from people who was no relation to each other but my thoughts was interrupted by Pa, whose train of thought was still chugging down its own set of tracks.

"Did I ever tell you girls how Phillip come by this farm?"

"Only dozens of times," Georgie murmured from her corner, stabbing at a seed pearl that wasn't cooperating.

I shifted Keely Faye's head from where she sagged against my arm. She started from her dozing, so I picked up the speed of my rocking again. "You prick yourself and bleed on that dress, Georgie, I don't know who'll be madder, Tandy, her ma, or you," I cautioned, always helpful. Georgie took leave of her concentrating just long enough to glare at me.

"He was rich, you know." Pa never paid much mind to our

smart mouths and evil looks at each other. "Well, maybe not exactly rich, but certainly pretty well-off. Made his living lawyering. Until about 1850, that was all Phillip did. Lived in a fine house in town, what town there was here then."

"What house, Pa?" It occurred to me to wonder if it was still standing.

Pa shook his head. "Don't know just exactly where it was."

It came to me of a sudden to wonder if it were possible Magnolia lived in my great-great-great-grandpa's house. I caught myself in a smile I didn't want to explain to Pa or nobody. If that was the case, I hoped my Grandpa Phillip took delight in haunting that awful lady every night.

Pa was still talking. "Where was I? Oh, yes. Well, one day, Phillip up and had enough of city life. Took this land in settlement of a debt, sold off his house in town, and moved onto this land with his wife, Esther, all his sons, and Deborah, his only daughter. Weren't much here then, 'cept a small house, some cleared fields, and three slaves to work it all. First thing Phillip did was free those slaves. Never did hold with the buying and selling of humans, he said, and wasn't about to start now. The three freed men stayed on to work the place for hire, and Phillip and his boys, who was actually most men by that time, planted the orchard and built them a mighty fine house down there by the creek. The house stood till Sherman came through. Ain't nothing but a cellar hole and chimney now."

Pa paused to scratch at his chin, as if he was seeing in his mind the cellar hole. From her chair in the corner, Georgie said softly, "We've seen it, Pa."

We had, dozens of times. It was just a couple acres behind

us, past the chickens, past the barn, past a sloping meadow where the cows grazed in the summer. Down over a little knoll too steep to plow or grow things on, then into trees. It was like stepping in another time to go into the quiet woods, where only owls spoke at night and the creek spoke all the time. That was where the house once stood, though now there was just the foundation left.

"He never knew the house was gone," Pa continued on, "since he joined up with the Confederate army, or what was left of it, the summer Joe Johnston lost all the land round Atlanta and was fixing to lose Atlanta, too, except 'ole Robert E. Lee had him replaced so it was General Hood what lost Atlanta to Sherman and the Yankees a few months later. Phillip was an old man then, but he got killed just the same, somewhere in the rifle pits near to what was left of the city, where he was defending his country."

"Why'd he join the Confederates, anyway," I asked, "since he hated slavery so much?"

"He wasn't fighting for slavery," Pa said. "He was fighting for his neighbors and his friends. He didn't believe in what they was doing, but he believed in them. And his land, *this* land, that had soaked up every drop of sweat he dripped onto it, then rewarded him with crops enough to feed him and make him rich besides. His neighbors, his friends, his land. That's why he went to the war."

"I still don't think it makes much sense," I said smartly.

"Lotsa things don't make sense," Pa answered. "The founding fathers, who wrote in the Declaration of Independence how everybody was created equal, some of them kept slaves. What it's all about, Mony, is that people face a time when they got to make a hard choice. Phillip was glad enough to see the end of slavery. But he felt he had to stand up for his neighbors and his friends, their homes and fields, the things they all worked for. By then, all anybody had left was each other. And, truth be told"—Pa sucked at his pipe and his eyes narrowed—"Phillip weren't the only southerner who freed his slaves and fought the war. Why, General Robert E. Lee, one of the greatest human beings ever lived, disapproved of slavery and freed his slaves before the war. As for the Yankees, hmmph. Ulysses S. Grant, the Union general who become president even if he didn't deserve to, his wife had slaves. Kept them all through the war, she did. So if you only look at the surface of things, if you only believe what people say, there's lots of stuff that don't make no sense. You got to look at the truth to see the sense."

Pa's voice kind of trailed off as he stared into the fire. I was sorry I brought it up, especially 'cause I wasn't sure I agreed with what Pa said. So I said, "What happened next, Pa?" I hoped Pa would leave off talk about the war and tell about the treasure. And he did.

"Phillip's oldest boys, Ezekiel and Rafe, was also killed in the war, same as their pa. Gabriel was took prisoner at the Yankee prison called Rock Island and never came home." Pa shuddered. "It was a terrible place. Anyway, Esther took Deborah and went to live with her kin in Charleston. The last son, Jonas, he was wounded twice, left his leg behind in a army doctor's tent near Shiloh. He was finally furloughed out and made his way home, arriving after the war was good and over. It broke his heart to find the family home burned down by Sherman, but with only one leg left, he didn't have no energy to spare and no money neither to build it back.

Besides, I don't think he coulda had the heart to build a house on the exact same spot that held so many memories of people now all dead and gone. So instead he built a little cabin on t'other side of the farm where he lived the rest of his days, scraping out a living just hisself, his wife, Orlinda, and their own two boys on this here same land."

"And the freed men?" Georgie asked, biting off a thread between her teeth. "What became of them?"

Pa rubbed his chin. "Well, maybe a year or two after the war, a couple of them started west. Got themselves a wife each, then took up with a wagon train going west to California. One died on the trail from some sickness. The other made it, 'cause he sent a letter to Jonas when he finally got to the Pacific. But that was all. Word didn't get around so good back then. Folks headed west and that was the last you heard sometimes. Anyway, Jonas hired back the third one, but that man weren't so healthy hisself. The war and starving took a toll on everybody, see. He stayed on only a year or two, then went to live with his growed daughter right in Torsten till he died.

"Jonas split his father's land in two, gave each of his boys, William and Robert, their own piece. My grandpa was William, and he lived in this here house we're living in."

"And Robert?"

"Robert didn't have no use for farming. He sold his half of the land to someone outside the family and moved up to Atlanta. William begged Robert to keep it in the family, but Robert wanted the money to start over somewhere else. William was cash poor right then and couldn't buy his brother out, but he didn't understand how Robert could just sell the family land. The brothers spent some years not speaking to each other 'cause of their disagreements over disposing of the land. But they finally made up their differences, knowing their own pa and his pa before him wouldn'ta liked a family quarrel. Phillip always said family was everything."

Pa stopped his talking, staring at the dying fire like he was thinking hard.

"The treasure, Pa," I prompted, my arms numb from the weight of Keely Faye, finally and fast asleep. I knew I should put her to bed where she could sleep proper, but I didn't want to rise up from my chair. The story always wove a magic spell around me, and I didn't want to break it until I'd savored every bit and even stored some up against the future.

"All right, all right. Let's see, where was I then? Okay. The story went there was a huge family treasure. 'Course it's all just talk. Except Phillip *was* still rich when the war started. There was talk he hid part of his riches before he went off to fight the war. He didn't tell nobody where he hid it. Must be he 'spected to come home to it, use it to make a new start when the war was done. But he never did come home, and the treasure, if there ever was one, is still missing."

"Do you think there was a treasure, Pa?" I asked, feeling little shivers on my spine like he was telling ghost stories. Which, in a way, he was.

Pa met my question with one of his own. "If there was, don't you think William and Robert and even Simon, my own pa, would have looked for it and found it?"

"And you, Pa? Did you ever look for it?" Don't know why I'd never thought to ask him this before. Somehow the story seemed so way back in the past it didn't have nothing left in it for us to touch or see, 'cept the old foundation by the creek. Now, suddenly, I realized the past, this treasure, was still living, could be somewhere and maybe could be found.

The little knowing smile Pa hid gave me the answer, but Georgie, in her corner there, didn't see the smile or catch the little twinkle in his eyes.

"Pa, did you?" Georgie echoed, still frowning at her threads and pearls and all that lace foaming up in her lap and falling round her feet. Georgie was too much a lady to be barefoot like I always was. I couldn't see her feet beneath the folds of fabric, but I knew that her ankles were crossed, her knees together good and dainty, and her feet tucked carefully away. Just like Ma woulda sat. There was comfort in the thought.

Pa laughed. "Maybe just a little. Just a little bit, I guess, because I knew I'd never really find it. No, the whole thing seemed a little silly, kind of a kid thing that I musta got over quick enough. If there was a treasure, someone would have found it long before me."

"So are you saying that there isn't any treasure?" I couldn't let the idea drop. I wanted to know for sure.

Pa hesitated, seeing how serious I was.

"With the war, most people lost everything just trying to survive, Sis. Money wasn't worth too much back then. Food was better than gold, and if anybody had any gold, they'da give it up in a minute just to get their bellies full. So, I 'spect there really wasn't any treasure hid."

I sighed down into Keely Faye's warm hair. That wasn't what I wanted him to say.

Pa felt my disappointment more than he saw it. He went

on, his voice as soothing as warm milk. "Well, now, my pa and his before him always said, far as they was concerned, what Phillip left behind was treasure enough."

"And what was that?" Georgie asked, putting the dress down so she could listen.

"Family. This land. The things he believed."

"That's not much of a treasure," I scoffed, wishing grown-ups wouldn't stray off into never-never lands of mushy sentiment. Why didn't they just stick with what mattered, real things, like gold and jewels?

"Someday you'll think different," Pa pronounced. "Some-day, even if this land were gone to strangers, even if we was poor and penniless and didn't know where our next dinner was hiding, someday all you girls will understand and believe in the treasure Phillip left you. 'Cause when you get right down to it, your family is really all you have. It's the only thing that matters."

Pa may have been right. But it didn't hurt to dream. I got up, careful as I could so's not to wake the baby, slipped quiet as a shadow from the parlor, and laid her in her bed. When I laid me in my own bed later on that night, when I finally fell to sleep, I dreamed of finding gold and silver and diamonds, all the kinds of treasure I wished Phillip thought to leave us.

One Saturday in May Pa came in from the morning chores as I was sweeping up the kitchen floor and thinking ahead to all the things there was to do. There was dirty laundry stacked to the rafters, and I didn't relish the thought of tackling any of it. The dust was building something fierce on top of dressers, under beds, in corners. No matter how I tried not to see it, I could hear it practically screaming out my name. Mama woulda died a shame to see what kind of housekeeper I was. It seemed sometimes mucking out the chicken coop, sorry as it was, might actually be preferable to picking up our own endless mess.

But when I saw Pa's face when he come in, it looked right proud, like he wasn't thinking about dust and laundry, but seeing how the kitchen floor looked good.

"Hurry that up, Ramona Louise," he sang out. "Then let's grab that grease bucket and that baby and go into town."

I hadn't heard such good news in weeks. Since Magnolia's visit, we'd all been working triple hard—Pa on the farm, Georgie on the widder's sewing, and me on the housekeeping. We'd hardly found a chance to do anything else. A trip into town was just what we needed, and I skipped as I hurried to tuck away the broom.

In no time at all we three were out on the road, walking

along the hard, oily dirt and drinking in the blinding bright May morning. We walked everywhere these days, partly because it was patriotic, and partly because driving the car anywhere didn't make much sense. The grease bucket would mean extra ration points for meat and cheese but not for gasoline, and we couldn't afford to be foolish with our precious, small allotment. Besides, the tires wasn't going to pass too many more inspections, and there was no sense in hurrying up the end of their usefulness. Especially when the day was as pretty as this one and town was only a few short miles away.

The birds was chirping, all the trees was in full leaf, and Pa so happy and our little family heading back to normal. The awful hole Ma left would always be there in my insides, but it wasn't such a cavern anymore. That pretty day, I could almost feel it shrinking up a bit.

The tornado was barely six weeks past us. A body would be able to make out the storm's half-mile-wide swath for years to come, but already the scars it left were healing up. The Hedgewicks' house sported a new roof, and McKenzie's barn, tore in half by the wind, was razed to the ground. Even the church, where three ladies including my ma were crushed under the rubble as they sorted clothes for Russia, was no longer a heap of busted boards. That mess had been cleaned up by the Boy Scouts. Pastor Wilkins said it would get built right back up again in its same old spot, so people in five or ten years could forget what happened and come to church not bothered by ghosts from what couldn't be helped. 'Cept I knew I'd never be able to sit in the new church and not be bothered.

Torsten only has one main street, and it was bare of cars

when we come into town. We passed the school all shut up tight for the weekend. The filling station cross the road was just opening up. I wished we would stop. Inside the little office was a red Coca Cola tub, filled with icy water and tall bottles of root beer and Coca Cola, birch beer and 7Up. I could almost feel the thick bottle glass against my teeth. I looked up hopeful at Pa, but he was pushing on and didn't notice. We rounded the curve past the little grassy park what held the war memorial and flagpole. The flag was up, flipping in the morning breeze.

It made me think of Adam. And Georgie.

Pa gave me some nickels outside the drugstore. "Take Keely Faye in to say hey to Georgie," Pa said, pointing across the street to the widder's shop where Georgie would be hard at work. I settled the baby onto my hip. "Then go get a sucker for her and something for yourself down at Gimble's." Pa straightened Keely Faye's little bonnet. "I'm going to the county ration office to get rid of this here grease."

I nodded, thinking ahead to the cheese and butter those extra ration points would mean. My stomach almost growled.

"Where you going after you drop off the grease, Pa?"

He rubbed his chin a little, and I could hear the scratchy whisker stubble. "I'm going to get me a shave and a haircut. You can meet—"

His words were cut off by a shout from down the street. We all looked toward the barbershop, just in time to see Harry Johnson get throwed out through his own big front window. Throwed right out behind him was a colored man I never seen before. They both landed in a pile of glass shards and commenced to bleeding.

It was as if everything was froze for a few seconds. Pa and me just stood there, eyes bugging out, like we was turned to statues. Then Pa sprung toward where the two men was laid out on the sidewalk.

"Don't move," Pa yelled as Harry Johnson stirred hisself. Then, "Somebody get a broom, so we can get these men out of here without nobody getting hurt worse."

Pa was so busy figuring how to rescue those bleeding fellas from the mess they was laying in, he didn't notice the men that came stomping out of Harry Johnson's barbershop to study what they done. There was four of them, and I recognized them all: Mr. Wade, who owned the cinema house, Mr. Farraday from the filling station, Mr. Taswell, who was on the city council, and Magnolia's Mr. Hewitt from the bank. Most of 'em was wearing Saturday clothes, but Mr. Hewitt was wearing his usual three-piece suit, with a pocketwatch hanging out of his vest.

"What's going on here?" This from Dr. Carter Fellowes, who till that moment was eating his lunch over at the cafe. The ruckus was bringing people out of all the stores along the street. Even the widder poked her head out from her shop clear down the street, and I saw Georgie slip past her and head our way. Somebody found a broom, and Pa was carefully sweeping the glass aside so's the two bleeding fellas could get tended.

Long with Harry Johnson's window, the Saturday morning quiet was all shattered.

And I was afraid.

"I'll tell you what's going on here." Mr. Wade stepped up to Pa. "This nigger was inside Harry's barbershop, getting hisself shorn. We done warned Harry about this, told him, Harry, your shop's in the white part of town. You gotta start obeying the laws around here. There's reasons for the laws, and this town ain't gonna stand by no more while you willfully disregard them."

"I think Mr. Johnson can decide who he will allow in his shop," Pa said, reaching a hand down to help the colored fellow to his feet. Dr. Fellowes was on the other side, pulling Harry Johnson up off the glass he was laying on. Georgie pulled up short and stood next to me behind the crowd, which was getting mighty thick for so early on a weekend.

"He can't do no such thing," Mr. Taswell bellowed. "This whole street is Jim Crowed."

He was right. Glancing up and down, I could see the little signs: WHITES ONLY. The colored side of town was across the bridge and railroad tracks. I never been down there, but I thought of a sudden it was pretty sure you'd never see a sign over there that said NO WHITES ALLOWED.

I commenced to shaking. What had Pa got hisself into? I remember stories, things I'd heard at school and once at the filling station while I was dipping in the Coca Cola bin for my birch beer. How Mr. Hewitt and Mr. Wade and Mr. Taswell and some other men I didn't know dressed up in sheets and burned crosses, beat up Negro folks and them what sympathized with them.

And Pa had plunked hisself right smack into the middle of 'em.

Taswell was going on. "All it takes is one fella violating the law, letting coloreds in to serve 'em, and the next thing you know the whole damn place's out of control." Taswell got right up next to Pa's face and hissed, "You want colored kids sitting next to yours in school? You want them beside you in the church? Well, this here"—he waved his arm toward Harry's shop—"this here's how it starts."

"Harry was warned," Mr. Hewitt added in measured tones. "He knew what was coming."

Pa didn't answer. He was too busy trying to soak up the colored fella's bleeding with a handkerchief.

"Better get 'em both over to my place," Dr. Fellowes said quietly to Pa.

Better get us all out of here, Pa, was what I was thinking. This was a bad thing to meddle with. A thing that gets your house burned down, gets you dragged out of your bed in the middle of the night to watch it burn and you can't do nothing . . . .

"Don't you touch him," Mr. Taswell yelled at Dr. Fellowes. "Them people got their own doc. If you know what's good for you, you'll just leave this all alone."

"And you better git your hands off of Johnson, too," Mr. Wade warned Pa. "This here's his own fault. Won't no law-abiding citizen have any more to do with him."

My hands was trembling so I feared I might lose a grip on Keely Faye.

Pa looked Mr. Wade square in the face. "What we have here are two injured people. I intend to do my duty, same as any other Christian man would."

With most of the blood wiped off his face, the colored man didn't look so bad no more. But Harry Johnson was a mess. The colored fella signaled Pa he could walk on his own, so Pa went over to help Dr. Fellowes, who was half carrying

Harry Johnson off toward his place. Georgie stepped back as they passed. I saw her watching Dr. Fellowes mighty close.

"You men are interfering with justice," Mr. Hewitt shouted after Pa and the doctor.

Pa stopped his walking and turned back toward the group. "Justice?" He shook his head. "This is cowardice, not justice."

"It's the law," Mr. Taswell protested, 'cept he didn't sound quite so sure this time.

Considering the good-sized crowd that was gathered, I was surprised Pa's next quiet words was so well heard.

"Maybe the law is wrong," Pa answered, his voice even and steady.

Mr. Hewitt drew himself up in righteous indignation. "Are you saying you're not willing to uphold the laws of this great state?"

"I'm saying I would've thought you four were better men than this," Pa said.

Dr. Fellowes gestured toward the nearly silent crowd. "There's womenfolk and kids here." His eyes rested just a bit on Georgie, then he turned his full attention back to the men. "You four go on home now, before this gets any worse."

Mr. Taswell stepped forward. "Who do you think you are, threatening us?" He didn't say "Yankee" but you could tell he was thinking it.

I clutched Keely Faye tighter to me, trying to still the shaking of my hands. Anybody touched my pa right then, I'd scratch their eyeballs out. I wasn't scared so much anymore. Just mad.

But my pa didn't even flinch. "Go home, Jack. The doc and me are gonna have our hands full enough with these two.

We won't have time to sew you fellas up as well."

"Why you . . . " Mr. Taswell clenched his fists like he was fixing to fight my pa. But quicker 'n anything, Dr. Fellowes stepped in front of Mr. Taswell, his face about an inch away.

"One of these days," Dr. Fellowes said, and I couldn't help but think he was sounding like a prophet from the Bible, "the folks in this fine state are going to declare clear and loud Jim Crow is wrong. Not right now. But real soon. And when that day gets here, because it surely will, the people watching you right now are going to remember this. How noble will they think you are then, with all your talk of law and justice?" He glanced behind him at the crowd, then fixed his eyes back on those four.

Shaming them.

"You're no better than the Nazis," the Yankee doctor pronounced.

Them folks didn't have nothing they could say to that. The broken glass and blood was telling them it was true.

All them men that was so full of mean words and tough talk couldn't seem to find a thing to say no more. A couple of them mumbled just a little, then they slunk off, back to where they come from 'fore this started. Mr. Hewitt had to pass right by me, and he glared at me 'cause of the grin full across my face. Didn't seem no need to cover up my mouth to hide it from him so I didn't, just grinned at him as he scowled at me a little longer than he needed to.

"Impertinent whippersnapper," I heard him grumble as he passed Mr. Taswell, and I wasn't sure if he meant me or the doctor.

Maybe it was disloyal to Georgie, but I had to admire Dr. Fellowes just a little bit.

The joy had all gone out of the day for me, and I was jumpy to get our business done and go on home. Pa couldn't get his hair shorn now, but after he settled Harry Johnson and the Negro man at the doctor's, he dropped off the grease bucket and we had our lunch at the cafe. The cherry pie was a nice change from poor man's cake, which was the only dessert we ever seemed to have anymore 'cause it didn't need no eggs. But it sure got a body sick of raisins. Keely Faye and I wanted to visit a few minutes with Georgie, but the widder hovered over us, all nervous we would muss her fabrics, so we didn't get much chance to speak.

Finally we left for home. Keely Faye was asleep in Pa's arms and Pa was silent, giving me a chance to think on all that had happened.

My pa and Dr. Fellowes was right for what they done. I was sure of that. But now it was over, my scaredness was overcoming all my pride. It kept creeping in my stomach, knowing that there was the Klan to think about, and what they do to folks. Pa's actions had made it clear as water he wasn't on their side. He'd put us all in danger, maybe, for all his talk about family being everything, not to mention betraying Georgie by siding with the doctor like he did.

We was halfway home that sleepy afternoon, and even the birds was napping. We was coming up on the river where it crossed under the bridge. I could hear it, still full up from spring and powerful.

Without knowing I was going to, I blurted out, "Why'd you do that for, Pa?"

"Do what?" Pa was startled, like he'd forgotten I was there.

"Why'd you take up for the doctor?"

Pa looked at me funny. "Dr. Fellowes? I didn't take up for him."

"Yes, you did. You jumped right in there, in the middle of folks you known forever, dressing them down like that, standing up for him that done what he did to Georgie."

Was that really what I meant to say? They tumbled out, the words did, and whether I believed them or not, they was said. My hands commenced to trembling all over again.

Pa stopped right there in the road, staring at me like I was speaking Chinese and growing two more heads besides. He shook his head slowly. "I wasn't taking up for the doctor. No, I was taking up for Harry Johnson." He looked at me sideways. "For Harry Johnson, and that colored man. For—" He started to say something else, but stopped. Then he added, "As a pa, I couldn'ta done no less."

Why couldn't folks just come out and say what they meant? Always beating round the bushes. Leaving sentences half unsaid, making people wonder.

But Pa kept walking, and I knew he wouldn't say no more about who he was taking up for. We went on a bit, then Pa added, "I should think you'd see that doctor ain't so wicked."

"I never said he was wicked. But you know, about Georgie, what he did to Adam."

"I know what folks is saying, but you shouldn't judge what

you can't understand." Pa didn't wait for me to argue, just went on. "No, the doctor's a right fine man, standing up like that for Harry Johnson and the colored folks."

"Hmmph," I said, because Pa had me there. "Well, *you* ought to stay out of those kinds of quarrels, least in public. There's never any good to come from getting in the middle of a fight with Mr. Hewitt and his kind. They come after people. At night, to pay 'em back for crossing them."

I shoved off in a huff, but Pa grabbed my shoulder, spinning me around. "Now, see here missy." The tone of his voice near frightened me. "Haven't I taught you nothing?"

I blinked, not sure what Pa was talking about.

"Listen up good, Sis, because I don't aim to say this more than once." He was so angry, his voice was shaking. I noticed for the first time his hand on my shoulder was cut, probably from picking glass off those two men. "I don't care who you got to stand up to. But don't you never forget. There ain't a speck of difference between the colored folks and us. They're all just people, same as white folks. They got hopes and dreams, broken hearts and worries, just like us. 'Cept maybe some of theirs is bigger, and if so, it's because of folks like them back there, people that got the wrong idea a couple centuries back, figuring anybody ain't the same as them can't be quite as good. It was the wrong idea then, and it's the wrong idea now. And the sooner us white folks get that through our thick heads, the better off this country and this world will be."

I hung my head, shamed I'd spoken. Pa had taught me those things since I was Keely Faye's age, and I guessed it only fitting she was sitting on his shoulders, woke up now, and wide eyed while he spoke.

"It ain't I don't believe you, Pa. It's just . . . a body gets in trouble saying those kinds of things in public. What if they were to come after you?" It was hard to say this last, on account of how near my voice was to breaking.

"If you can't bring yourself to say such things in public, you must not believe them very strong," Pa answered, now gentle, realizing fear had made me speak, not hate. "When you don't stand up for what's right, you're casting your vote for the wrong. 'As for me and my house, we will serve the Lord,'" Pa quoted.

I wondered what serving the Lord had to do with Jim Crow laws, so I thought it over for a minute, thinking quick back over all the sermons Pastor Wilkins gave and all the sermons my pa taught just by the things he did. I got more out of my pa's living sermons than the pastor's spoken ones.

"You mean"—I kind of fumbled through my thoughts, putting them in order right out loud—"being truly brothers with everybody, sticking up for people no matter what side of town they's from, that's what serving the Lord is all about?"

Pa nodded. I stood there, rolling it over in my head. It was a big thought—that just being *people* made us family, not blood, nor skin neither.

"But Pa." I hustled to catch up, as he had started off again, leaving me standing there, thinking in the road. "But Pa, even if it is so wrong what people are doing, what good can just one or two people ever do? You can't change the world."

"Oh, but we can," Pa said, almost joyfully.

"How, Pa?"

His answer was simple and full of hope. "One barbershop at a time."

CHAPTER SIX

Pa's words stayed with me all the way home, all the rest of that Saturday, and through supper when Georgie didn't have a bad word to say to Pa about him standing up with Dr. Fellowes. She didn't have *any* word about the whole thing, just a halfway prideful smile on her face when she kissed Pa good night and gave him an extra-long hug. 'Course, if I was waiting for a sign from her of admiration over Dr. Fellowes, I woulda had a long wait, 'cause she didn't have a single word for him neither.

It got to finally be June. No more school for a while, and weren't nobody gladder than me. With gardening, the always-dirtied dishes and clothes, the house, and minding Keely Faye, I still found bits and pieces of time when I could put my broom down, leave the clothes hanging on the line to dry, and slip into the woods. Down at the creek there was a dozen ancient trees I could sit beneath and dangle my toes in the creek to cool. The old foundation was there, too, and it didn't take too much imagination to turn back the clock a hundred years.

It was a golden time. We was all busy, barely seeing each other till supper time. But the farm was sprucing up and my dinners getting tastier, and it was like we was all in a cocoon, where the rest of the world couldn't touch us.

But there was times, late at night, when Georgie was breathing deep and steady cross the room, I couldn't keep myself from thinking on my ma and remembering how dreadful much I missed her. And sometimes it weren't too big a stretch from that, 'specially with the darkness leading me on, to drift to worrying about Mr. Hewitt and what would happen if he took it in his mind to be teaching my pa a lesson. It's easy to get stuck in thoughts like that when your mama's dead, and wicked folks is thinking blackly on your pa and he's all you got left. The worry turns to scaredness, then to terror, then your dreams get populated with the stuff of nightmares. If I got yanked awake by faces of a dreamed-up Klan, I'd lay and shake and feel cold sweat soaking in my sheets and pray without daring to move an inch that no harm would ever come to Pa.

In the end it weren't the Klan that killed my pa, though.

It was the bull that got him.

The wicked, hateful bull Pa was keeping in the pasture at the end of the lane from the house. I hated that animal like I never hated any other thing. He looked at me when I had occasion to pass by as if he harbored all the evil in the world, nurturing it until in his full wrath he would lash out and destroy us all. Which he nearly did.

Pa liked to take Keely Faye sometimes to see to farm things, 'specially in the cool of the morning when the birds was rejoicing. He'd made a contraption he could strap onto his back to carry Keely Faye around while he did the morning chores or even drove the tractor. It was kind of like what the Indians carried their papooses round in, and Pa got a kick out of wearing it, keeping Keely Faye right close to him. Pa even tied on a couple of her little toys so if she dropped them, they wouldn't be going anywhere and she could grab them right back up again.

That June morning Pa was chopping wood, and he had to take Keely Faye off his back for that. Pa musta laid her down underneath a tree to sit and watch him working and play with the grass and butterflies. She probably dozed off. Then I guess he decided to lay down with her for a little snooze hisself before he finished up his work. He carried a long, fat, red sash in his pocket for such occasions, which he tied round his leg, then around hers so if she woke up 'fore him, she couldn't get too far. I guess he didn't take sufficient care tying it that day, though, 'cause when I looked out the window while I was filling my mop bucket in the sink, I could see her little yellow jumpsuit bobbing, with her in it, toward the bull pasture.

I grabbed up Pa's shotgun, fearing for the worst. If she got inside that pasture that bull would tear into her soon as he saw her. I took off toward my baby sister at a dead run, praying the bull would somehow overlook her.

I don't know how she got past the barbed wire, but there musta been a place where the bottom strand was pretty high. When I saw Keely Faye in her yellow jumpsuit toddling through the tall grass inside the fence, I screamed at her. My screaming musta woke up Pa, 'cause next thing I saw he was running toward her hisself.

But now so was the bull.

Pa throwed himself under the fence right fast, and he reached her 'fore the bull did, scooping her up in his arms, then turning and running back toward the fence, that stupid sash trailing from his leg. That bull was charging right behind, and I could see it was gonna be close. Raising up the shotgun to my shoulder, I wished I was a better shot.

The recoil 'bout laid me flat on my back, but I fought to keep my feet and did.

I nicked that beast's shoulder, but instead of being proud, I realized with horror it was probably the worst thing I coulda done. 'Stead of killing him, I'd just shot out his shoulder, filling it with buckshot and him with rage.

Pa and Keely Faye were almost at the fence when the bull reached them. I was closer now myself, raising up the gun to give the monster the other barrel when Pa slowed down to throw Keely Faye over top the fence where he hoped she'd be safe from the ton and a half of running rage behind them. She hadn't hardly left his arms when the bull tossed Pa over his shoulder. It was the most awful sound to hear my pa land kind of behind the bull and to the side, crumpled in a busted-up heap. But there weren't no time to think on it. While the monster got hisself turned round, I fired again. I got him in the neck this time.

But it was too late.

When I scrambled under the wire and knelt beside my pa, I knew he was already dead.

It was Keely Faye's crying finally brought me to, and I looked over to where she landed. She was laying on her face and shoulder, which would later show purple bruises. Her collarbone was broke from the awkward landing, but I didn't think nobody would fault Pa for that. Throwing her saved her life, and it slowed Pa down just enough to lose his.

"It's not fair. It's just not fair."

"Hush, Mony. You'll wake up Keely Faye."

"Keely Faye's not here. She's at the hospital."

Georgie sighed. "I forgot."

It was hours later, nearly midnight. All the neighbors had gone home and left us. The sheriff and the ambulance and the pastor and all the folks that showed up at our place to inspect what happened to our pa were gone. Dr. Fellowes had took Keely Faye away, said he would give her something for her pain and to help her sleep, and we could have her back tomorrow.

We were supposed to be asleep. That's what they told us: "Now you girls get yourself some sleep, you hear?" Like all we was waiting for was their permission. Like orphan girls could go to sleep alone in their house, just like that, after what happened to their pa.

"Don't you hush me!" I didn't want to shout at my sister, but I couldn't stop myself. "What are we going to do? We're all alone. There's nobody to take care of us."

"There's each other. We still have each other."

I sat up on the bed where I'd been crying for too many hours to count. I pushed my tangled hair out of my face. It was all mussed up with tears and stuff from my nose and even dribble from my mouth, 'cause I'd been laying on my face and crying for so long. Georgie helped me sort of smooth it all and I looked up at her.

Georgie was all that was left now to take care of us. I remembered all the nightmares about Pa leaving us. Well, he finally done it. Just me and Keely Faye, and Georgie left to take care of us best she could.

Which sprouted new and awful thoughts . . . now what would happen if Georgie, too, were gone?

Not dead and gone, 'cause surely with all we'd been put through God would not allow another death.

But there was still New York, Paris, London, Georgie's dreams, to worry over.

A sixteen-year-old girl was most a lady, and a lady with big dreams that a baby sister and an awkward kid like me would hold her back from. She'd be gone right this minute, I was betting, 'cept for us. 'Cept for the leftovers of her family, which was us, and all the burden that put on her shoulders.

I wouldn't think about it. Didn't need no more disasters to fret over, not till this was past.

"We're in a frightful fix," Georgie whispered, holding my head against her chest, her other hand rubbing my back. "We're in a frightful fix all right," she repeated, "but we'll be okay. We'll just get us through this first night, then we'll be okay."

She kept repeating it over and over, kind of like a lullaby. It was Georgie's way of facing things, saying it over and over made it not so bad. If she could say it enough times, she could lick it. I fell asleep while she was still saying it, and as for when Georgie finally fell asleep, it must have been real close to dawn.

That's how we got through that first night.

Georgie said we had to get things back to normal quick as we could, or we'd have folks interfering in our lives and grown-ups trying to take us over. I remembered when the Picketts' mama died in that train wreck and the state people came and scooped the whole lot of those orphan Picketts up and they disappeared. I didn't want us to disappear, and neither did Georgie. From the way she pulled her chin up, pasted a smile on top of her grief, and put herself in charge, she made it plain from the first my worries of that night Pa died were to be put away. This was our home, and she was aiming to make sure everything stayed put. Specially us.

Weren't five days after Pa died, Georgie was back to work. We decided, for the summer anyway, I'd keep house and watch over Keely Faye. Georgie'd work for the widder, and we'd do the farming chores together, 'cept the garden, which was left full up to me. We didn't say it in so many words, but both of us determined to do better than anyone in town at keeping things together. We had only one more chance to make our family—what was left of it—work out, and we didn't aim to lose it.

$\mathcal{A}$ few days after Georgie had gone back to work, I plumb ran out of Mr. Clean and blueing both together. It made a good excuse to skip the wash and leave the floors unmopped, but the kitchen floor was sticky in some spots and I couldn't abide that. So soon as things was picked up after lunch, I washed my face, put a blue dress and bonnet, both sprinkled with flowers, onto Keely Faye, stuck her in her carriage, and set off for Gimble's.

A few weeks ago I made this same walk with Pa. It was surely different now. The very air seemed changed. Lifeless.

We have to go on, I told myself. There's no choice to the matter. We have got to go on living in this world, no matter we are orphans now. Keely Faye don't deserve to grow up in a mournful house, believing there weren't any happiness to be had no more. I reached down in my soul and tried to summon up a smile. It felt false and pasted on, but for Keely Faye, at least, I needed to start smiling again.

An hour later we was in town, me pushing Keely Faye and her sitting up wide eyed and watching houses pass us. We'd just pulled up in front of the drugstore when down the street I saw the widder marching along, her thick high heels clunking on the sidewalk as she turned into the hairdresser's.

"Can you believe the luck?" I asked Keely Faye, who was

facing me, her eyes protected from the afternoon sun by the pulled-up carriage top. "The widder'll be in there hooked up to that hair-frying contraption at least a couple hours. Let's sneak down into the shop and say hey to Georgie. The widder won't come out till her hair's all blue and frizzy, but we'll be long gone by then."

Keely Faye gurgled, blew a bubble, and set her arms to smacking at the air. I laughed and pushed the carriage to the widder's shop.

It was cool and gray inside, without no lights on except what came in through the plate glass of the giant windows. Georgie was in the back, pinning a paper pattern to a bolt of rich, yellow fabric the exact same color as a buttercup. She looked up at us.

"Why, look," she said, as if she were talking to someone in the shop with her. "It's my two favorite sisters, come to say hello."

She smiled at us. Weren't nothing false or pasted on about her smile. I wished I could look so genuine happy. Georgie had a way with doing that.

"Wow," I breathed, touching the soft yellow folds of fabric. "This is awful pretty."

"Yes, it is," my sister agreed, stuffing pins into a cushion hooked around her wrist like a bracelet. "I almost hate to cut it."

"Who's it for?"

Georgie pushed a thick black curl behind one ear. "Mrs. Bumperstockings."

"Who?" I felt my face scrunch up as I tried to place the name.

Georgie pointed with her elbow and I turned to see what she was showing me. "Mrs. Bumperstockings. The mannequin. As soon as this is finished, I'm going to dress her up in it and put her in the window for everyone to see. Won't they just be green, to see her wearing something so fine?"

"I hope you're going to give her new shoes, too. Something strappy. And a pretty hat."

"The best."

"Has the widder seen this?"

Georgie shook her head. "No, I'm not letting her till it's finished."

"What's it going to look like?"

Georgie didn't look at me. In fact, she didn't look at anything. Just tried to pretend it was no monumental deal. "It's just a design I've been working on. I'm hoping it turns out okay."

Turns out okay? How could Georgie's dress be less than stunning? The only problem with it would be that it did not belong in a shop like this, on an ancient, chipped mannequin among the drowsy duds the widder took such liking to. Georgie's dress belonged in New York. Or Paris.

Anywhere but here.

Someday . . .

"That dress she's wearing now"—my sister gestured at Mrs. Bumperstockings, staring at the wall with the same wide-eyed, surprised expression she had worn so many years— "goes in the box. I'm going to ship it off as soon as possible. That frightful dress will never sell, but the widder can't see that. Look at it." She pointed with the scissors. "The color is no good. Nobody looks good in orange like that. It bunches at the waist, and the bosom is all billowy and lopsided. The collar's puckery and tight and looks like an afterthought. The sleeves are silly. Long sleeves with cuffs for spring? Whoever heard of that! No, it will never sell. It's been in the store since 1941, for heaven's sake."

I took Keely Faye out of her carriage so she could poke about exploring, then I wandered around the worktable to get closer to that buttercup cloth. "What box?" I asked, idly running my fingers across the fabric again and again, wondering how anything that weren't a cloud could be so soft.

"That box," Georgie gestured toward the store's front. "Beside the register."

I leaned over the table to see. It was an ordinary pasteboard box, about the size of a washtub and nestled up against the table where the register was perched. Some clothes hung over the edge, not new and crisp like those for sale, but somewhat faded out and worn. A fish-colored blouse topped the mournful pile.

"Whatever is the box for?" I said, not really caring as I turned back to watch Georgie start to cut. I think we both held our breath as the scissors parted all that buttercup.

"I told the widder it would be a good thing to do, not only for the drive, but to get people in the shop. We're asking people to come in here with their old things, stuff they won't use no more. They donate it to our clothes drive, and when we have enough, we'll pack it all up and ship it off."

"Ship it off where?"

Georgie straightened up, her cutting done. "To the Russian people, those that survived Hitler so far. Things are awful over there. They have nothing left, they're refugees with no homes, no food. Remember? Ma was . . . "

Georgie's voice trailed off when she saw my eyes. I stared at her a long time, thinking of a heap of broken boards and Remmy Mack crying out.

"How can you?" I shouted.

I didn't mean to shout. It startled us both, and Keely Faye, sitting on the floor playing with fabric scraps, whimpered, scared.

"The Russians didn't kill our ma, Mony," Georgie answered with her voice all gentle. "It's not their fault and it wasn't hers."

"If she'd stayed to home that day, with us where she belonged, 'stead of worrying about those folks across the world, dying for them. . . . She should have been home worrying about her own family!"

I was screaming and crying, both at once. We was in the back room, but the couple lady customers wandering in the widder's shop could see if they'da mind to, and I didn't care. Words and tears came pouring out of me, words I hadn't even thought about before but now I saw they'd been there all along. Until the bull I was so busy being strong for Pa I hadn't realized that I was angry at Ma. I was angry at the war and the Russians and the tornado and the church, everything that had conspired to take her away from me. I was angry, so very angry at my ma. My pa, too.

Because they were gone.

"Mony." Georgie's voice was sharp as scissors and it cut through me just like cloth. "Ma was just trying to do right. That's all she ever wanted, just to do right. It wasn't no one's fault what happened, and there had to be a purpose to it. We don't know what, but there always is a purpose. That's God's way. Ma was just trying to do right, and Pa, and now I want to carry on for them."

"Do right?" I kicked the box. "Is it doing right to worry more about those foreigners than you do about your own kin? What will you do next, sweep up me and Keely Faye and put us in a box and send us off somewhere, to some deserving person who doesn't have kids because that's right?"

The awfulness of what I'd said stunned us both. I felt Georgie's eyes fixed on me, but I could not look at her. Till that spot in time, I would not have believed I could say such a thing, could *think* such things, but it was said and my words hung between us in the air, like they was a possibility. In the room was just the sound of my thick, heavy breathing. Then Keely Faye commenced to crying, kind of soft and scared. Her crying picked up steam as we stood there, me panting like I'd just got done not drowning, Georgie staring at me still stunned from what I said. I yanked my baby sister up, grabbed the carriage, and flung us toward the front door, out of that shop fast as I could, kicking the box of clothes out of my way as I went past.

I was so upset when I left Georgie I plumb forgot what I come to town for in the first place and was going home empty-handed as well as mixed up, grieved, and tore to bits inside. I couldn'ta said exactly what was all the feelings in me then—didn't seem right to be mad at Ma, who was dead, and Georgie, who was not. I knew it wasn't anybody's fault my ma died, not really, and blaming those poor Russians wasn't any more right than blaming Ma. I didn't dare be mad at God, though it sure seemed He coulda done more than he was doing for the world in general. I guess He had his reasons, but they didn't make no sense to me.

Kicking all those hurtful feelings round my gut, I managed to get me and Keely Faye home. The sun was hot, but that wasn't what made my skin feel all crawly. It was an awful walk.

I was stirring a pan of grits for supper when Georgie got herself home. I'd gone from feeling awful to not feeling much of anything. It was a trick I learned. Not feeling much of anything doesn't hurt like feeling awful. It was easier, even though I knew someday the awful feelings would catch up with me again like they did at the widder's. Catch up, and eat me up alive.

"Mony."

I knew she wanted me to turn around but I didn't. Facing her, I'd have to face everything.

"Mony, I know it's hard for you. It's hard for me as well. Sometimes I just want to dig a hole and get inside to stay forever. Sometimes I guess I want to die."

I squeezed my eyes shut tight as they could go. Don't die, Georgie, don't ever die. If you leave me and Keely Faye, there will be nothing left. Nothing.

"And when I want to die . . . ." Her voice trailed off, and I felt her hand squeezing my shoulder. "Those times, I think of you. You and Keely Faye. All I have to do is think of you and all that wanting goes far away." She paused. "I'll never leave you, Mony. How could you think I'd ever want to send you away?"

When my big sister put her arms around me and I felt her

tears mix with my own, I knew I had been unfair to Georgie. Unfair, wrong and downright mean.

We was sisters, and we always would be. Keely Faye and Georgie and me. Nothing ever would separate us.

Pa weren't gone no more than a few short weeks when Magnolia showed up on our doorstep again. The house was finally emptied, after all the time of putting up with church folks and neighbors being helpful, bringing pies and loaves of bread and pots of beans to us. Pastor Wilkins near wore a path between town and us, coming by every day, wringing his hands worrying what to do about us orphans.

The sheriff brought some lady from the state out to talk to us, asking us if Pa had a will and who was supposed to raise us now he was gone. I kept my mouth shut, just kept my eyes glued on Georgie, sitting dignified and grown-up-like on the needlepoint parlor chair while the lady and the sheriff sat on the couch together. My fingers was all knotted in my fists, the nails digging tunnels in my palms. All we needed right now was for Keely Faye to set up a yelping if she woke up from her nap.

I was a wreck of nerves, but Georgie answered real polite we could raise ourselves, since we didn't have no relations we knew of but had a house and farm left to us from our great-great-great-grandpa Phillip Thomas Keddrington. Georgie told that lady how she had a job and, between us, Keely Faye wasn't hardly a handful. The state lady said something about an orphanage for Keely Faye and me, but Georgie got right indignant at that and said we was a family and we'd stay together and that was that. The lady said she didn't see how it could be allowed, but the sheriff and the lady and Georgie talked for quite a while that day, and I didn't catch much of the drift except some stuff about a petition to the court and seeing if Georgie could be appointed our guardian even though she wasn't quite seventeen.

I don't know how Georgie could sit there and talk so calm. Our pa was gone; our ma was dead. Couldn't Georgie see those folks was fixing to parcel us out to separate places where we might never see each other again in our lives? My heart was thumping something furious in my ribs from being scared to death. I felt like a firecracker, fixing to blow up. It was all I could do to hold myself back from screaming.

Then I looked down and saw Georgie's white clenched knuckles. I studied her face closer. Georgie's pleasant smile was no more natural than the sheriff's teeth. Her face was so tight that it must have hurt her hair.

Of course she could see the possibilities. That's why she was making herself be calm, so they'd think she was a grown-up. So they'd think she could be our ma.

I lifted up my chin. I commanded my fingers to relax, my heart to stop its reckless thumping. I felt right grown-up my-self, of a sudden, figuring it out. I wouldn't scream, wouldn't make a sound. I would show that lady I was a well-brought-up girl, like Georgie, and didn't neither of us need no orphanage so long as we had each other.

It took a whole long hour, but they got it ironed out some-how, "for now," according to the lady, and finally left us alone.

And that's when Magnolia showed up.

"I couldn't live with myself if I didn't make certain that darling baby receives a proper home and real parents now both hers are gone," Magnolia said to us piously, teetering herself into the parlor without waiting to be invited.

That darling baby was still snoozing in her bed up in our room, and I was petrified Magnolia would just whisk her away somehow. I glanced at Georgie, but she didn't look a bit concerned.

What she looked was mad.

Magnolia trilled on. "It wouldn't really be like splitting you girls up, since you and Ramona would both be welcome to come visit Keely Faye at our house once in a while, especially at first. I'll have my lawyer draw up the papers at once. You may be assured she will receive all the love and care she needs." Here Magnolia drawed a big sigh and dabbed herself with a little lace hanky. "I declare I never understood why the Good Lord did not see fit to bless me with a child of my own. I do believe I see His hand in this, providing me this chance for a child after all."

How nice Magnolia saw God's hand in letting that bull kill our pa so she could steal our baby. Georgie's eyes was spitting fire but she hadn't put her words together yet, so I decided to jump in. "Pa already told you to mind your own business, Magnolia Hewitt. So why're you back here, troubling us in our grief?"

Magnolia struggled to keep that phony smile stuck to her face. "Things are different now, Ramona Louise," she replied. "Even your pa would agree, that baby needs parents, adult parents, and you girls are simply not old enough to care for her. It isn't right for you to even try. I'm making this offer now, hoping to head off the tragedy that will otherwise occur when the authorities are forced to parcel you out to an orphanage or various homes, since goodness knows, no one in these difficult days will be willing to take on three extra children just like that. Don't you see you will be split up, separated, never to see each other again? This way, you have a chance at least to be close by and remain acquainted with each other. I'm doing you a favor, and I think you should be pleased."

"You're not doing anything but helping your own self." Georgie found her voice at last. There ain't nobody better than Georgie in a crisis, I was finding out. Which was a real good thing, considering how many crises we was having lately. "You may take your favors now and leave," she continued, all calm and dignified, "and please don't bother us again."

Magnolia, on the other hand, weren't much good for nothing, in a crisis or out of it. She just grit her teeth to keep from shouting as she leveled a cold and steely glare at us. "You are both ungrateful children. All right, then, because you are so stubborn. You will receive one thousand dollars. Each."

"In exchange for our sister?" I asked, incredulous. Was that all a life was worth?

"Mrs. Hewitt, if a price could be placed on that child's head, neither you nor anyone else on this earth could touch it if you possessed every ounce of gold and diamonds there was," Georgie responded evenly, cutting off my splutterings. "Now you may take your pitiful bribe and your shameless self out of our home and don't ever trouble yourself to return or we'll bring the story of this conversation to the sheriff and you will go to jail for trying to buy a child."

The woman drew herself up righteously. "I did no such thing. Who would believe such a story? I only offered, as a Christian and a neighbor, to deliver you from your difficult situation. You have no idea how wearing it is to care for a child. You're deceiving yourselves if you even think it is possible. This is no situation for two children such as yourselves, and someday you will thank me for what I will do in raising your sister."

I would have lunged at her at that, 'cept Georgie musta read my mind. She had me by the shoulder 'fore I could tear into Magnolia, holding me back. Spite of that, she wasn't riled the least. "You'll not raise her, Magnolia" was what she said. "We'd rather die than give her up to you."

"Choose your words carefully, Georgianna Keddrington. You forget who you are talking to."

"Threats never frightened my pa," Georgie replied. "And they don't frighten me, either. So you may take your threats and leave now. If you don't, Mony and I will swear out a complaint against you and you'll have to answer to the judge."

"The sheriff will never believe two children."

"Are you willing to take that chance?"

Apparently Magnolia wasn't. She drew on her gloves, favoring us with what she hoped was a scorching look as she headed out. "This is not the last of this. I can ruin you," she shot out just before I slammed the door, barely clearing her rear end as she took off.

When she was fully gone, I looked at Georgie. Her face was pale and she was breathing a little harder than I would have thought was necessary.

"We're not afraid of her," I assured Georgie, forgetting just for that second we were alone in the world.

"No, we're not," my sister agreed. "But we can't underestimate her, either. She's right she can make a lot of trouble."

We had to go to court. Halfway through June, the lady from the state came back and gave some legal papers to Georgie, summoning us to court so a judge could decide what was to become of us. Our court hearing was in the last week of June, and Georgie said in our case, the fact there was a war was a good thing. 'Cause of the war, lots of the men was gone and there was more than the usual number of widows and orphan kids. The state people was having a dickens of a time trying to take care of all the kids that didn't have nobody. Lotsa people still wanted babies, but nobody wanted us big girls, Georgie most seventeen and me going on thirteen.

We fixed up Keely Faye right smart. She was growing so, she'd busted clean out of all her dresses, so Georgie whipped her up a new one, made from a flour sack but you couldn'ta told. Georgie smocked the yoke with ribbon left from the making of a Sunday dress for Mrs. McKenzie down the road. The ribbon transformed the cheap, rough fabric into something much too pretty to describe. Keely Faye's hair was growing in gold and beautiful, and I fussed with it till it like to glowed.

If we'd had a little diamond-crusted crown, you could believe she was a princess.

Georgie fixed me up to look like a princess, too. She took

one of the dreadful, draggy dresses left from the widder's dusty inventory, sliced off a strip of skirt, and ripped out the suit-like sleeves. She used that strip of skirt to make a fitting collar, tucked and basted the deep navy cloth, cut out new gathered sleeves, and put the fabric back together for a whole new life. When I put myself into it, I nearly gasped out my delight. It was drapey now, and beautiful, just right for a young girl on a high summertime day.

Georgie'd even brung me home a hat from the shop. "Just to borrow," she warned. "We can't afford to keep it." But I didn't care. I never much understood hats before, but when Georgie put that borrowed one upon my head and turned me to the mirror, I almost couldn't breathe. Maybe Pa was right and I would grow into my looks.

"What are you fixing to wear?" I asked her, pulling myself reluctant away from my surprising reflection. I'd been so consumed with Keely Faye and me, I hadn't thought too much about Georgie.

"I'm wearing Ma's best dress," she answered quiet. "I thought it fitting."

And it was. When Georgie came stepping careful down the long staircase pulling on her gloves, I felt like crying. Ma's dress, the one she only wore to church on Sundays, was meant for Georgie now. It was deep forest green, with a yoke and collar made of tatted lace. Georgie'd pulled her hair up, clipped into soft curls that fell below her ears and lay respectful against the little collar. Fixed to the bodice was a brooch, the cameo Catalina Hortense Simmons wore on her wedding day, a gift from Phillip's mother. Georgie, always beautiful, but never more than now, was transformed. She was like Ma, but more. She was Ma, Pa, Catalina, Phillip, all those folks rolled together ready to take on a judge, ready to keep her family together.

It was something to behold.

At the bottom of the stairs, Georgie smiled at me. I wanted to tell her what she'd done to us, to make us all so beautiful and respectful, so prosperous and content. But I didn't know the words, and I was afraid of doing a disservice to my dress by sounding silly. So instead of saying anything, I just stood there like a post. Georgie smiled and put her arm around me.

"Don't you worry," she breathed into my ear when she felt my shoulders start to shake with tears. "No judge would dare to split us up today. Look at us. You and Keely Faye so beautiful. We belong together. No one can dispute that now."

"You are magic," I whispered to her shoulder, feeling Ma's dress against my cheek. "You done magic with us all. Just like Ma would, if she was here."

"She is here," Georgie told me, and I knew it was the truth.

It was a long, hot walk to town, and when we finally reached the steps of the courthouse, all the happiness and confidence had dribbled out along the road from home.

"It would be best to let me do the talking," Georgie said, straightening the slipping hat back on my head.

For once, I didn't smart mouth back. I let her do the talking for us, 'cause she was Georgie and she was smarter and I didn't want to have to speak in front of all those folks. Truth to tell, I didn't think I could. Most normal days if I worked hard ironing and scrubbing floorboards, I could almost forget my parents was both dead. But no matter how I tried to push it all away and go on living, sometimes it came back to me and I got right heartbroke. I didn't have to wonder what would happen there in court if I got thinking 'bout losing Georgie and my baby sister, top of all else that was gone.

Magnolia was there, decked out in her finest, just like us. She told the visiting circuit judge she was an old family friend (lie) and could offer a loving home (bigger lie). Then she broke out her little hanky, heavy with lace, dabbing at her eyes like she had a heart and sobbed how it broke her up she couldn't have no babies of her own. She said she'd step in and do her patriotic part, relieving a small part of the government's orphan troubles by taking little Keely Faye in, raising her and loving her like her own.

She didn't offer to take us.

Georgie stood up to her. Made me proud to see her, standing there telling that judge how we was family and belonged together. She told him how we had the farm and her job for our support, how we lost our ma and pa, but before he went Pa taught us how to work hard so's we could always stay together. She shot a look at Magnolia which sent that woman quaking in her size five boots. Georgie's look dared Magnolia to blabber to the judge how it was Pa's fault he died and Keely Faye got hurt, 'cause Magnolia knew Georgie could do some blabbering of her own. Judges don't look too kind on the buying and selling of babies.

Or threatening people out of 'em.

The lady from the state told the judge a bunch of stuff that made no sense to me 'cause I wasn't listening much. I was shaking enough for all of us, holding Keely Faye on my lap, trying to keep that hat from falling off my head and praying like I never prayed before. Please, God, keep us all together, please, God, please. I woulda prayed to Mary, too, and all the saints, 'cept we wasn't Catholics and I don't know much about that kind of praying. But if I thought it woulda helped, I woulda prayed to the sun, the moon, and the stars, Jupiter, Zeus, and Mohammed, too. Anybody who mighta been able to do us a lick of good.

Whether it was all that praying that I did or Georgie looking so grown-up or just the good sense of the judge, we got to stay together. The lady from the state told us we was all in Georgie's custody, her being almost an adult and impressing the judge how responsible and mature she was. But next she told us it was only temporary, kind of like probation, what criminals get. We would have six months to prove ourselves, and people from the state would come snooping round our house, making sure we was clean and eating right, that Keely Faye was getting took good care of and we weren't suffering none. If, at the end of our six months' probation we was all still fine, then we would never have to worry about the state no more.

When it was done and over, my legs was shaking so I couldn't hardly walk. We took the trolley most of the way home, only having to walk the last bit after the end of the line. I had to keep stopping to rest and still the shaking. Finally Georgie pulled me to her. We didn't say no words, just cried like babies there by the side of the road, getting all the worry and grief out of us, putting it away where it couldn't do us no more harm.

"We're going to be okay," Georgie told me, solemn-like. "We can do this. Just like Catalina Hortense Simons did."

Remembering our great-great-great-great-grandma now squared up my shoulders. Her blood was flowing in my veins, figuratively speaking anyways, and thinking of her courage was all I needed. The shaking left. I tossed Keely Faye up on my shoulders like Pa used to, and even though she bounced something frightful up there, we trotted that last half mile, itching to get started on our new life together.

We had beat Magnolia, and had won in court, at least for six months. We surely didn't expect trouble to come from the widder Baxter. For the first time in her business life, she had got herself some help and things was looking up for her store. So why all of a sudden she took it in her mind to quit, I couldn't guess. She didn't offer any explanation, just Georgie came to work one day and found a CLOSED sign on the door and everything locked up tight.

Georgie hunted down the widder and found her, rocking in a swing on her front porch. "I'm tired" was all the widder said, and went back to her rocking.

It weren't near the tragedy it woulda been, if Georgie were anybody else. But Georgie weren't no quitter who'd sit down in the road and cry when things didn't go her way. From the time she was five, sitting at Ma's feet handing up scissors, Georgie did always want her own fashion designing career.

In spite of the widder's being clammed-up tight at first, by the end of the morning, she and Georgie reached an understanding. Georgie marched herself over to the court building, where she spent a couple hours filling out papers and talking fast, and came out with a document saying she was an emancipated minor, which meant she could sign legal stuff and people had to treat her like an adult even if she wasn't. Then she went down to Mr. Hewitt's bank, and before the day was over we had us a mortgage on the farm.

The mortgage made it possible for us to own the widder's shop. But it was the first time since Phillip Thomas Keddrington laid eyes on that land there was a piece of paper saying someone not a Keddrington had a claim on it. I 'bout lost my supper when Georgie 'splained it all to me.

"You mean to tell me you *gave* this farm to Mr. Hewitt?"

The sausage gravy and biscuits, just about my favorite thing to eat, near choked me. I pushed my plate away so I would not be tempted to throw it at something.

"No, that's not what I mean to say at all," Georgie said, cool as cucumbers while I considered smacking her. "It's just a mortgage. Mr. Hewitt took the farm as collateral in exchange for giving me the money to buy the widder Baxter's shop."

Collateral? I looked at Keely Faye, dipping her spoon into that gravy and smearing it across her shirt. Sometimes I wished I was little again. Didn't seem right girls like us should be troubled about mortgages and collateral, fixing our own meals, and raising a cow and chickens while we figgered how to pay for a dress shop.

Georgie was going on. "The money I earn at the shop will

pay the mortgage back and clear the claim the bank holds on the farm. And then we'll own it all: three hundred acres, two sheds, a barn, and Mrs. Baxter's dress shop besides. Except first thing tomorrow, I'm going to change the sign. To 'Keddrington's.' Remember?"

I nodded, remembering Georgie's dream, feeling just a little scared. Things was happening too fast for my liking.

"What are we going to do about the farm?"

Georgie bit her lip. It was the first time in all those awful weeks she looked uncertain. "I don't know. Maybe we should lease it out. I don't know just yet. For now, we'll just . . . just try to keep up. Keep our garden going, milk the cow, do what we can. Together. And we'll see."

I nodded. She went on.

"I'm going to teach you how to keep the books. You may not be much for grammar, but you got a head for numbers, and even if you're young, I think you can manage some of the business aspects of the shop. I'll handle the buying and the selling and the seamstressing, just till we can afford to hire us employees. Then we'll find a bigger building, expand our line to men's and children's things, and pretty soon we'll have the biggest, best clothing store in Georgia, maybe all the South."

"But how can you be the best if you can't study like them other fashion designers in New York and Paris?" There I went, saying the first thing popped in my head. I clapped my hand over my mouth soon as I spoke.

But 'stead of crying like I woulda done, Georgie squared up her shoulders and straightened her back, just like Catalina woulda done. "I don't guess I'm going to go to New York or Paris for a while," she breathed, and I knew it was the first time she'd brung herself to say the words out loud. "But if I can't go to Paris and New York, they'll just have to come to me."

I didn't know how she expected to make that happen, but I figured on helping her every way I could.

Business was real slow at first. Everybody in Torsten and its surrounding parts was working at the factories and the mills, burning off their energy and coming home so tired they didn't care to shop. Even victory gardens was taking up their time, and when the railroad opened up line gardens, letting folks plant crops 'longside the tracks on railroad company land for free, nobody had time for anything but weeds. They said the war was near to over, but it weren't over yet, and I guess people didn't think it fitting to have new clothes and stockings till the guns was quiet.

Still, we did some business here and there—neighbors who wanted to see us do well, mostly; maybe some felt sorry for us, too. Even Dr. Fellowes come in a couple times and bought hisself some dresses.

"Saw this in the window," Dr. Fellowes said, as he pulled out his wallet to pay for a pretty pink shirtwaist. "It will look terrific on my mother, and her birthday's coming up."

I didn't let on he'd said the same thing the week before when he bought three blouses and a slim black skirt. I just punched the buttons on the cash register where I was helping Georgie so's she could do a fitting in the back and wondered did the doctor buy them things because he pitied us or 'cause he really did want them for his mother up north.

Georgie managed to make the first mortgage payment. She also bought and sewed herself a fine new line of clothes for the store for the fall season. She spent most of her time in back, whipping up some dresses out of her own imagination, but she wanted to keep them out of sight till enough new stuff was ready so's we could have an elegant grand opening, complete with little cakes and tea and Torsten's first-ever fashion show.

We'd had lots of our own vegetables growing nice and steady in the Georgia sun until the heat got to be too much for them. I watered the cucumbers, squash, and melons every day, trying to keep them from splitting open and their vines from drying up. But with the little business here and there at the dress shop, we wasn't too worried about getting by. We wasn't worried, that is, till the warm July day I went into Reese's General Store for some supplies. We was low on everything 'cause I always put off shopping. I was so busy every day, helping at the shop as well as all my work at home. All that milking the cow, begging the squash and carrots to please grow some more and the weeds to grow some less, mopping, dusting, fixing meals, all that work plumb wore me out and I didn't have no stomach left for shopping. I hoped the state people wouldn't come snooping round too soon. If they peeked in the cupboards 'bout now, there'd be some fault to find.

Keely Faye was walking pretty good by then, toddling beside me as I found the stuff on my list. Mr. Reese tallied it all up at the front, and I instructed him to put it on our bill, just like he always did.

Instead of smiling like his usual self, though, Mr. Reese

hemmed and hawed some, rubbing his chin. His actions was puzzling to me, but his response was lots more puzzling.

"Can't do that, Mony. Can't do that anymore."

I blinked a couple times. I couldn't have been more confused if he was of a sudden speaking Portuguese to me. Or sprouted tusks like a walrus. It was like being in one of those dreams where you open your mouth to say something and don't nothing come out but a squeak. I swallowed a couple times, then tried my voice again.

"What do you mean, you can't do that? We've always charged our things. You know we always pay up."

"Well, it ain't like always anymore, I'm afraid. I understand you got yourselves a mortgage on that farm now. We can't extend no credit to people what's got themselves a mortgage."

"Why not?" I was trying to be real grown-up and businesslike, but it was getting harder by the second. In my mind there was a picture of our pitiful bare cupboards. We had some early vegetables, but no bread or flour, not even grits, and no way of getting any.

Mr. Reese's face changed a little as he saw my panic. He looked around the store as if he didn't want to be overheard, then leaned over the counter toward me. "It ain't my doing," he whispered. "But we got a notice from the bank just yesterday. See, when I order things for this store, sometimes I do it with a loan from the bank. And the bank told me yesterday they can't secure my loans anymore if I extend too much credit to people that might not pay because things was so tight they had to get a mortgage."

"But we always pay," I wailed, not thinking of the other

three or four ladies wandering among the shelves, not caring now who heard.

"I know that. But the bank has set new rules, and they won't give me any more money if I don't abide by those rules."

The bank.

Mr. Hewitt's bank.

"Mr. Reese," I asked, gathering my wits about me and trying to sound casual. "Did the bank mention us by name in particular, as folks you couldn't extend credit to?"

He rubbed his chin. "I don't guess the bank's got any thing against you Keddringtons special, but you kind of were mentioned in particular. That's how I knew about the mortgage."

That Magnolia does know how to twist an arm, I told myself, full of sudden hate. She musta known how hard it is to start a business and figgered on starving us out. Well, we'd show her a thing or two.

I straightened up my back. I was growing so, I could almost look Mr. Reese right in the eye. It felt good to be near tall as an adult. "Thank you very much, Mr. Reese. I won't be buying anything today, I guess." I picked up Keely Faye and walked on out of there, leaving all our necessities behind.

I picked up Georgie at closing time. "Let's don't take the trolley home," I commanded as Georgie carefully locked up Keddrington's.

"I'm tired, Mony," Georgie answered shortly, digging in her purse for our fares.

"We have business to discuss," I told her, steering her and Keely Faye away from the trolley stop. "And we won't be taking the trolley home much anymore for a while."

There. That was pretty grown-up-like. I tried to smile, but Georgie heard the strain in my voice. "What's this all about?" she asked as we tromped across the street and headed out toward home.

"Magnolia's been meddling in our finances," I told Georgie as we made our way along. "We can't get us no more credit at Reese's."

"What's Magnolia got to do with Reese's?"

"Well, since we got us a mortgage, Mr. Hewitt decided Mr. Reese can't give us no more credit. It's cash on the barrelhead from now on for us. And, since there ain't no cash, we won't be getting any groceries."

Georgie didn't ask me to go into details on why there weren't no cash. She didn't need to. Everybody in this town did business on a credit basis, including Keddrington's. In spite of the mill and the factories nearby, lotsa families still depended on cotton and crops for their cash money. At harvesttime, in two months, everybody in the town would be rich. Everybody paid off all the credit they'd took out the rest of the year to tide 'em over till the crops was in. The biggest part of the year, most all the farming folks lived on credit. Mr. Hewitt knew that.

"So what are you planning on us eating for the next two months?" Georgie asked it like she thought I had an answer. That scared me a little. Usually it was Georgie who figured things out. But since I started keeping the books, she was treating me more like we was partners. Like I was older than I was. Like I was smart. Like she had confidence in me.

I turned it over in my head a spell. "Well, we got us our garden. And our cow."

'Course, flour and grits don't grow in gardens. And unless we slaughtered the cow, meat would be hard to come by. But I couldn't let Georgie down. Georgie and Keely Faye.

"And there's the chickens," I added brightly, though I knew we needed to keep on selling the eggs to help pay the bills.

Georgie was tired after the long day at the dress shop. That was probably the reason she was not finding all the problems with my answers to what was staring us in the face. "We only need to get through the summer," Georgie said. "Just through the summer. Can we live on what we can grow that long?"

I didn't think so.

"Sure," I told her, not wanting to disturb the confidence she was showing in me. "Mrs. Hedgewick told me they don't have a garden on account of Mr. Hedgewick's arthritis and both their sons is off to the war and she is taking full-time care of their farm. She asked if we could trade some vegetables to her for fresh bread and pies now and then. And there's berries still that I can pick, and peas and spinach and tomatoes from the garden already put up. With milk and bread and eggs, we can get by. Maybe I can get her to throw in some jam now and then. You know how much you like bread and milk if there's raspberry jam to drizzle on it."

"Will we have enough milk and eggs?"

I didn't think so, but I nodded enthusiastically. "Georgie, don't you worry a thing about what we'll eat." I was trying to be soothing, like my ma. "You just concentrate on that store, getting dresses made and sold. Remember, that store is what will pay the mortgage. I'll take care of what we'll eat, and we'll make a good team."

My words were a lot more brave than I was. Maybe we *could* get by on what we could grow. But it wouldn't be easy, specially now it was so hot and would probably take a lot more work than there were hours in the day for. Pa always said a person could accomplish more by working smarter, not harder. If Georgie 'n' me could figure out ways to work smarter, maybe we could pull this off. But it could get right hard to fool the state people into thinking we were doing just fine, and we couldn't pay that mortgage with only our good intentions.

We walked the rest of the way home pretty quiet. I don't know what Georgie was thinking, but I sure was wishing somehow we was rich.

We rounded the last corner just as the late sun touched our windows, gilding them like they was made of gold. I almost laughed. We didn't have a penny to spare, but our house had golden windows. It made me think of Phillip's treasure.

It was silly to dream about things that couldn't be, but I couldn't help but wish there really was a treasure. Because we sure could use it now.

Great-grandpa William Keddrington built his farmhouse tall and square, with a long wide stairway leading up to four big bedrooms in the upstairs. There was a bedroom in each corner, the stairway making a great deep hole in the middle. Georgie and me always shared a room, from the time we was little girls, and now we moved Keely Faye's little bed in with ours. Didn't seem right to have her sleeping in a room all by herself when me and Georgie was sleeping side by side. Even with us all together like that, since we was orphaned and became alone, most nights I couldn't sleep, and whether it was the muggy heat or nightmares kept me up, I couldn't tell. I heard a lot of things those nights: owls and ground creatures warning each other off back in the woods, big frogs and the voices of night things carrying sharp and clear through the dark. Times the moon was out, the light fell through the big, low window, sharp and white across the bare wood floor-boards of our room.

When the window was so full of light, it drew me to it, out of bed and cross the floor. There was a rocking chair and rag rug set right there, and I'd push the rocking chair aside to kneel down on the rag rug one of my grandmas made. I'd rest my elbows on the wide sill and lean out, listening, looking at the garden down below, the little barn and lane, all washed in the strange, blue brightness of the summer moon.

It was more beautiful than any words could say, and I thought sometimes I'd stay there all the night. 'Cept sooner or later I'd fall into too much thinking. Then I'd shiver, even when the day'd been too hot to stand for. I'd shiver, feeling of a sudden all lost and lonesome, wishing myself sick for Ma and Pa.

That night I woke up to see Georgie standing in the window, which was full to bursting with the moon's bright shining. Her shoulders was convulsing and she had her fingers balled up against her eyes. I never seen Georgie cry like that before, not even when her soldier boy was suddenly gone off those months ago.

I laid there watching, praying she would stop. It took for-ever, probably near ten minutes, till her shoulders finally stilled. Even then, I waited some more time before I spoke.

"Georgie . . . "

She turned, not surprised, and not embarrassed, either, to find me watching her. "Go back to sleep," she said, her voice croaky, like the frogs out in the night.

"I can't."

She sniffed and sighed, then turned back to the window. I heard her voice come at me cross the room, real soft.

"I know. Me neither." She nodded toward the barn, the garden, and I saw for a minute how hopeless it all was. I felt my heart thumping in my chest, heard it thumping in my ears.

If Georgie was scared, I was scared.

What were we going to do?

Her words were like she could hear my thoughts. "Whatever made me think we could do this? We're just a couple of kids. A baby, a farm . . . in the daylight, it don't seem so bad. But at night, when I look out this window at this place . . . It's so big and scary. So much bigger than us. How can we do this?"

She's just tired, I told myself. Just tired and worried. I didn't want to believe, couldn't believe, that she would give up.

"We can do it," I told her, like maybe saying it would make it true.

"I wish I could be near as sure as you sound."

"Just take it one day at a time," I said, thinking it was just what Pa would have said.

"But are we doing right by Keely Faye? Are we really?"

This answer was easy. This answer weren't just wishing it was so.

"Georgie, there ain't no one in the world could do better

for her than us. You don't ever have to wonder that again 'cause you know it's so. She's right were she belongs, with us. We're her own flesh and blood."

Georgie closed her eyes and swallowed. The way she hugged herself together with her arms looked like she was afraid she'd fall to pieces if she once let go.

"Maybe Keely Faye really needs a mama, a real mama. Not a couple of big sisters playing house. That's all we are, Mony, we're playing house. Except we got us a real live baby and a real live farm to tend. What that baby needs isn't us. It's a real mama."

Everything was now clear to me. Georgie was in a dark place. She needed me to show her the way out. It gave me strength. "Georgie, Keely Faye has a mama, watching over her from Heaven."

"How can that be enough?"

"And she's got us."

"Oh, Mony. We can't do this." She stretched her hands out, almost helpless, almost giving up. "Look at this place. We can't do this. We need a grown-up."

I lifted up my chin. "I bet even Pa wished for a grown-up now and then."

"Pa was never scared of anything in his life."

"We can't be scared," I pleaded. "We won't be scared. We just won't think about it."

"Look at Keely Faye." Georgie padded softly over to our sister's little bed. Looking down at her sleeping face, Georgie breathed, "Sometimes I can see in her face how much she wants her ma. Oh, Mony." Her voice broke in two. "Oh, Mony, I want my mama too."

What to say to that? In the silence of that night, it could seem Georgie was right. We needed a grown-up. But there was not one to be had.

Just for that night, I decided to pretend. I'd be the grown-up. That's what I was thinking, and that's how I figgered I had to sound. If Georgie needed her ma, I'd be her ma.

What would Ma say to this? I only had to think a moment 'fore I knew. I knew it was what Ma would have said, because what came to me sure didn't come from me. It wasn't nothing like what I woulda chose to say.

"You want your mama? Well, you can't have her."

Could that be me talking? I was being harsh, even mean. But it felt like the right thing and I plowed ahead. "You can want your ma all you want, but she's gone and won't never come back."

Even when I saw in my sister's eyes how I was hurting her, I didn't let up. I couldn't let her fall apart. If Georgie lost her gumption now, there'd be nothing left. Only Georgie could save us. And only I could save Georgie. So I pushed on, hating the words but knowing somebody had to say them and there was only me to do it.

"There ain't nothing fair about it, but the way it is, is the way it is. So you can stand here taking cold all night and wishing. Or you can climb back in that bed and pull them covers up to your chin. You can turn up on your shoulder like you always do and go to sleep. 'Cause tomorrow's coming, and we both have work to do."

The shock and hurt in Georgie's eyes was too big to look at. I crossed the room to her, took her shoulders in my hands, and turned her, nudging her toward her bed. She let me push her off the rug and past the rocker, cross the wide boards of the floor to the bed where she slept. I sat her down, picked up her feet, and turned them onto the bed, then pulled up covers over her.

She let me. And she lay there, looking up at me and trusting me. Like I was Ma.

I leaned down to my big sister and kissed her forehead. Just like Ma would.

CHAPTER TEN

I left the shop mostly up to Georgie, and she left the farm mostly up to me. Doing the books only took a little time, so I had plenty to give to the house and garden. But even with as much attention as I was giving it, our food situation got dismal mighty fast. Ole Tess was getting stingy with her milk, which made me afraid she meant to go dry on us sooner than we planned. I feared for the chickens, too. A few of them took sick and died. I read the agriculture pages of the *Atlanta Constitution Journal* every day, discovering to my horror there was some dread chicken disease with a huge long name going round and farmers was losing their whole flocks. I hoped that wasn't what I was seeing here, but in the absence of another explanation, it kept me up at nights, along with everything else that was worrying me.

Even the garden, which I labored so with, was turning on us. It started out real fine, but as the summer wore on, I noticed signs of critters. Coons and rabbits was stealing in at night, chewing up the foliage, eating stalks and leaves right down to nubs. And then the crawly things come in, and between the awful heat and the cutter bugs and worms and other stuff I didn't know nothing about, we lost most everything. I worked my fingers raw with what was left, even sitting up nights on the porch where I could keep my watch, Pa's old shotgun cross my knees. At least the melons was doing pretty good, and I didn't aim to let anything happen to them, if it meant I had to stay awake till Christmas.

What milk there was, Keely Faye got. Eggs too, after what we sold to the co-op. The peaches would be ripe pretty quick, and that would help. Mrs. Hedgewick told me she was anxious for some beans to put up, and I spent most afternoons searching through the few tomato plants left, picking off whatever bugs I could spot. It near made me throw up, though I couldn't tell if it was the nausea that comes from never getting much to eat or the squishing worms what did it.

I worried lots over Keely Faye. Her cheeks was thinned right down, and she got real whiny. 'Course, me and Georgie felt pretty whiny ourselves. But then one morning Keely Faye woke up feverish and lay listless, hardly moving while I rustled up some breakfast that she wouldn't eat. Worried, I felt her little forehead. It was burning. A sudden, terrible thought took hold of me. Was this what polio was like? Was Keely Faye going to die?

We didn't have no money for the doctor, but she sure needed one. I laid a folded-up blanket in the basket that was wired onto my sorry old bicycle and squished the baby in on top of it. She was too big for the basket, but I didn't have no choice. We had gas ration stamps left, but we didn't have no cash to buy gas with. So I peddled us into town fast as I could. Keely Faye didn't even seem to notice how cramped the space was. Seeing that only made me peddle faster.

It felt funny walking into Dr. Fellowes's place. Last time I was here, Pa was with me.

Pa.

I wouldn't think of that, I told myself as I leaned the old bike up against the porch and ran into the house with Keely Faye.

The clinic took one half of Dr. Fellowes's house; his living space filled up the rest. It was an L-shaped place, with two front doors. It felt like walking in somebody's house without a knock, but it was easy to forget the feeling once inside the door. It smelled like the floor was scrubbed with alcohol. There was an old long couch with metal legs, three metal chairs, and two stuffed plastic benches that looked like they came off a bus. Somebody stuck ashtrays the size of dinner plates on end tables holding lamps, and scattered all about were *Life* magazines and some yellow *National Geographic*s.

Dr. Fellowes didn't have no nurse or secretary to greet patients so we just sat ourselves in a corner, away from the door in case someone else came in and didn't want to catch what Keely Faye had caught. The door that closed off the waiting room from the place where he did his doctoring of patients was shut tight, the faintest murmur of voices squeezing out underneath the wooden panels.

It was ten minutes before the door opened. "Thank you, doctor," a lady I'd never seen before cast over her shoulder as she stuffed a handkerchief into her pocketbook.

"Don't wait so long next time," I heard the doctor scold from back inside his room.

"You're right, of course. I didn't want to bother you."

"Pneumonia sometimes starts out like a simple cough, Mrs. Freschette. It's not a bother, believe me. This is what I'm here for."

She nodded, pulling the door closed. After glancing at us once, she disappeared out the front door.

It was our turn.

Dr. Fellowes poked and prodded. Keely Faye just lay there looking forlorn. When he was done listening to her breathe and peering at her eyes and ears, I pulled her shirt back on over her head, waiting, scared, to hear what he'd say.

I near cried with relief when Dr. Fellowes told me Keely Faye wasn't fixing to die just yet. "It's not infantile paralysis, I'm certain of that. Her throat is fiery red, though. See those white spots down behind her tongue? I think it's strep. It's never good, but she should recover. You were right to bring her in."

It left me weak, I was so glad to hear she wasn't going to die from polio. I sat down hard in a chair, realizing my hands and knees were shaking.

"You feel okay yourself? You don't look too perky." He laid a cool hand gently on my forehead, checking for signs of fever.

Him touching me like that, even if he was a doctor, brung all my feelings into my throat. Nobody laid a hand on my head that way before 'cept for my ma. But she was gone, and so was Pa. We were broke and hungry, and Keely Faye was sick. I broke down sobbing like Keely Faye shoulda been if she wasn't feeling so poorly she couldn't even cry.

"There, there." He was patting me on the head. It only brought more tears. Having that man sit beside me, telling me not to cry, brought back how much Georgie and I were alone with our troubles, how much we could use somebody grown-up to take care of us. I wished it wasn't Dr. Fellowes trying to comfort me. Because he had sent Adam Carbee off to war and broken Georgie's heart and I wanted to be mad at him. I didn't want to like him, but remembering him that day with my pa standing up to those Klansmen and feeling him now beside me patting me and helping Keely Faye get well, I wished Dr. Fellowes was a friend instead of our enemy like Georgie considered him.

He waited till I was all cried out before he spoke. Then he put his arm around me and hugged me just a little. There wasn't anybody in the whole town I could trust, but here was Dr. Fellowes, suddenly so kind, hugging me as if he was my pa. I found myself crying all over again and blubbering out all our tribulations to him. And he listened, not embarrassed like lotsa folks woulda been, but real caring-like.

I blurted out the whole story—how Magnolia couldn't have no baby and was so misguided to think she could have ours just for the asking. I said how Magnolia aimed to get Keely Faye by shutting off our credit, forcing us to starve or give in. I told him how Georgie got a mortgage on the farm Phillip Thomas Keddrington built up more than a hundred years ago. I told him how Georgie's shop didn't have no choice but to keep extending credit and she didn't expect people to pay their bills till the peaches and the apples and the other crops was in. I told him how we was living off our dismal garden and our drying-up cow and chickens, but pretty soon we'd either have to cave in to Magnolia or starve to death. I told him how the people from the court would come snooping around any day now and we'd be sunk when that happened 'cause there weren't nothing but the salt and pepper shakers in our cupboards. And I told him how scared I was Magnolia was gonna win.

"I had no idea," Dr. Fellowes murmured, then murmured it again. "I had no idea. What you girls have been going through!"

I was stricken with a sudden fear. He could go to those state people and blabber everything I told, that we was starving and Keely Faye was sick. Maybe he was supposed to, being he was a doctor and all; maybe he had an obligation to report such things.

As if he could read my mind, the doctor started talking.

"It's all right," he said, in a gentle, reassuring voice. "What you just told me will be kept a hundred-percent confidential. Even if I wanted to, which I don't, I can't ever tell anybody. For any reason. Doctors, and ministers, too, have a special right when it comes to people's secrets. In fact, it would be against the law for me to tell anybody else whatever you tell me."

I glanced at him through my blurry tears. He looked sincere and mighty caring.

The clock ticked for a few minutes while I composed myself. Then, feeling just a bit embarrassed for crying on his shoulder, I figgered I'd better gather up Keely Faye and go. But he wouldn't let me.

"Now don't go running off just yet. So far, you've been doing all the talking. I guess it's my turn now." He smiled. I settled myself back in the chair, curious, and he went on. "I guess you girls are in a fix all right." Dr. Fellowes stared off into space. "So what are your options?"

Options? We didn't have any. I shrugged. "I guess we'll just keep on doing what we're doing, long as we can do it. Then one day a big car with the seal of the State of Georgia painted on the door will pull down our lane and the people from the state will show up to snoop. We'll be like old Joe Johnston's army, outflanked and having to retreat. Magnolia will get Keely Faye after all, Georgie will lose the shop, our family's home will be taken by the bank, and we'll be out on our ear with nothing, no place to go. Except I'll get took to an orphanage, I guess. Georgie, being the emancipated minor that she is, will be left all on her lonesome to fend for herself."

Dr. Fellowes did some more thinking, then asked, "What do you suppose would have happened to old Joe Johnston if he had got those reinforcements he needed so bad?"

Joe Johnston? The Confederate general? What did a Yankee know about all that?

I shrugged. "I guess he woulda stuck it out, maybe even beat Sherman."

"Maybe what you need, then, is just what he needed. Reinforcements."

I smiled at the idea. "Where would we get reinforcements from?"

"From your friends."

I didn't want Dr. Fellowes to know we didn't have any friends, not real friends anyway, since Betty Barber moved up to Raleigh and Kel Ceasar's pa took the whole family off to California. And Adam Carbee went off to the war. All we had now was neighbors who had their own troubles to tend to.

"I don't think we can expect much help from friends" was what I said instead.

"I think you can." His answer was quiet and firm. "One of them, anyway. I know I'm not much, but I'd like to be your friend."

Funny how my throat could close up like that. I didn't know if it was telling me to laugh or cry. The idea of a friend like Dr. Fellowes was tempting. He seemed so capable, so sure of himself. But it was impossible.

I sighed. "I don't think Georgie would like that much."

"You're probably right." He nodded solemn-like. "I can't think of anybody in the whole United States of America that dislikes me as much as Georgie does."

It gave me the opening to ask the question that had so long been heavy on my mind. "Then you really did send her beau away?"

"So they say," Dr. Fellowes said, his voice sad and resigned.

"Harry Johnson says you're like David in the Bible, what sent Uriah to the war hoping he'd get killed so he could take his wife Bathsheba for hisself," I prompted.

The doctor smiled, but not like anything was funny. "I guess it would kind of look that way. I did make rather a fool of myself when I first came to town, not knowing Georgie was already spoken for." Dr. Fellowes shook his head a little, remembering. "She was the prettiest thing I ever saw. I guess I just lost my head about her."

He stood up, clasping his hands behind his back, and sort of paced. I wasn't used to grown-ups talking to me like that, 'bout stuff so personal. I didn't know what to say.

"I know what Georgie thinks," the doctor went on, "and I don't blame her. I know what people are saying, and that's okay. It's just a grown-up thing, Mony. You wouldn't under-stand."

"I'm near grown-up," I protested, looking down at Keely Faye, who had fell to sleep right in my arms. "And Georgie's got herself a paper from the court saying she is full grown-up. Can sign papers and everything."

"Georgie's quite a girl."

She was, I had to agree. I remembered those times Dr. Fellowes came to see Georgie before he knew she was sweet on Adam. He'd brung her flowers, then sat with her on the porch for a long time, talking. The time he brung her candy, she set the box aside on the wide ledge of the window and they walked down to the peach orchard for a while. He woulda kept coming back, too, except she finally got him to understand it was no use, 'cause of Adam.

And Adam joined the army only one week later.

It was plain Dr. Fellowes still loved Georgie. I didn't think it was disrespectful to Adam Carbee's memory, even if he was alive somewhere, to admit that Dr. Fellowes would have made a fine match for Georgie, if it had worked out that way. Still, a man who sends another off to war . . . surely it weren't right, though it was near impossible to believe the doctor had. He seemed too nice to do something as low-down mean as that.

I guess a man must hurt an awful lot when his heart was broke. I wondered if it was too much suffering to live with, made him go irrational sometimes, like I thought grief was doing to me.

"Either way, I guess you're right, though, Mony." Dr. Fellowes, interrupting my thoughts, had come full circle, back to what got us started off like this. "If Georgie knew I was the reinforcements, nobody'd blame her for being upset. So we can't let that happen, can we? This is too important."

I nodded uncertainly, not sure where he was headed with this.

"Tell you what," he said, and I took new hope from the decisive tone of his voice. "Will you let me help you girls out now and then? It has to be our secret, just you and me. No one else can know, Georgie most of all. Okay?"

I nodded, still not sure what he meant. How could he help out? He'd already bought all the dresses he could pretend were for his mother's birthday, and Georgie would surely see him if he tried to weed the melon patch. But I didn't feel as hopeless as before.

"What about Keely Faye?" I asked, the heaviness in my arms finally reminding me of the reason why I came.

Dr. Fellowes wrote out a prescription. "Take this over to the drugstore. She should perk up pretty fast. Let me know if she doesn't."

I stared at the prescription. How could I pay for it?

It took him just a couple of seconds to realize what straits we was in. Then Dr. Fellowes reached into his pocket and pulled out his wallet. He took out three bills, which he pressed into my hand.

Now I understood how he could help.

Dismayed, I started to protest, but he shushed me.

"You're in the middle of an emergency, Mony. This is an emergency loan, that's all. I'm going to make sure you pay it back, so you don't have to worry about it being okay to accept it. Keely Faye needs that medicine, so you just march yourself over and buy it. Remember? I want to help. Just don't tell Georgie where it came from."

I looked down at the money he'd put in my hand. I'd never thought a Keddrington would have to accept a borrowed handout, even in an emergency. I felt pretty low, but I didn't know what else to do. Keely Faye needed that medicine, and there weren't no other way to get it.

My head argued with my guts, but my head finally won. Reluctant, I closed my fingers around the money. "I don't know when I can pay you for today, either," I mumbled.

"I've got a suggestion for that, too." Dr. Fellowes rubbed his chin again, and I could see he did that pretty regular. If a day came when he had too much thinking to do, he could near rub his face right off.

"I'm a terrible housekeeper. A pretty good doctor, if I say so myself, but a terrible housekeeper."

He'd sure hit that nail on the head.

"I'm getting plenty sick of eating all my meals at that cafe, but I haven't time to cook. I'd be really grateful for somebody to clean my house once a week, maybe cook me up a roast and a pie and a couple loaves of bread now and then."

I opened my mouth to butt in, but he held up a hand to stop me. "You could bring Keely Faye, and listen to the phonograph while you worked. That way, you wouldn't have to pay me a thing for today; you could work it off instead. And when we're all even, I'll give you a salary so when this war is over you can go out and buy yourself one of Georgie's best new dresses. Be the envy of all the rest. What do you say?"

I didn't know what to say. He was offering to save us, just

like that. I couldn't hardly look at him, my insides were so confused. Before I looked up again I pasted a smile on my face, but my heart was in my shoes. How could I do this to Georgie and not tell her? How could I not do it and hope we'd stay together?

CHAPTER ELEVEN

Keely Faye perked right up once she got that medicine working in her, and I started working for Dr. Fellowes three days later. He wasn't stretching the truth any when he said he wasn't much for housework. Looked to me like instead of washing socks, he was going out and buying new ones every time he took off a pair. I never seen so many socks, and they was everywhere—under the bed, under the sink, even on the kitchen drain board.

"Good thing the state people ain't snooping here," I muttered to Keely Faye as we stood in Dr. Fellowes's kitchen that first day. He didn't seem to own a single pot or pan to cook in except for frying pans, of which he had seven. There were no mixing bowls in his cupboards, and the only food was cold cereal, a couple jars of peanut butter, and half a jar of homemade jam that looked to have come from the pastor's wife. She'd given us a jar just like it when Pa died, but it was long gone.

I set to work, making up a shopping list, gathering up the laundry and running it through a Maytag washer which was considerable newer than ours and had a clever removable wringer thing which looked like it had never been used yet. It took most of the day, but when it was time to go, there was four loaves of bread cooling beside a berry pie and stew bubbling on top of the stove.

Dr. Fellowes weren't back yet when I was ready to go. I peeked into the empty little clinic joined onto his parlor. He'd had patients in for two hours in the morning, then took his old jalopy car to go make house calls, and I hadn't seen hide nor hair of him since then. I wished I could see his face when he saw his folded laundry, clean socks, and sparkling kitchen, with the pie cooling sitting there all proud beneath the window. Not this time, I guessed. But there'd be other days. Whistling, I packed Keely Faye up on my back and we skipped down the street to Keddrington's to pick up Georgie.

When we got home, there was a grocery bag full of apples, cheese, potatoes, and carrots tucked up beside the front door. I figured Dr. Fellowes thought he was pretty sneaky, leaving stuff like that, but chard and summer squash don't fill up a body's gizzard none too good, so I sure wasn't complaining. I didn't let on to Georgie who brung that stuff, either, though she was a sight puzzled over it. "Musta been a neighbor, feeling guilty for not helping us before," I said, and shrugged. I hauled that bag inside the house and whipped us up some applesauce and scalloped them potatoes. At dinnertime, we ate like royalty.

Next time I went back to work off more from our debt, Dr. Fellowes asked me if I'd dust his clinic and scrub the floor and windows. As soon as he took off, I set to work. The phonograph in the parlor was a wonder, and I hummed along with the music coming out of it while I polished up his windows. I was almost finished dusting and was thinking ahead to the floor when I saw a stack of files sitting on top of the doctor's desk.

I could see without trying how there was names on all those files—Hodges, Hedgewick, Taswell, even the widder. I kind of touched them, just a little, thinking how truly interesting it would be to peek a bit inside. But I didn't. I turned away and kept up my dusting, finished that, then started on the floor.

Those files just sat there, daring me to set my rag and bucket to the side and take a little breather. Them files were yelling out my name, and I couldn't stop myself from finally giving in. I was tired from all my dusting and scrubbing, so I sat down in Dr. Fellowes's chair. I only thought to spend a minute peeking, just a bit, not really reading anything I shouldn't. I bet there ain't a kid in this whole world who woulda done different.

I touched the top file, tracing the writing on it with my finger. *Clancey Family* was wrote on a little tab. I knew of the Clanceys. They lived outside of town, the other way from us. Mrs. Clancey suffered from consumption.

It wasn't really snooping, I told myself. If these were secret, they should be locked up. Besides, I wasn't going to read them. I was just kind of flipping through to see who all was in there.

Dr. Fellowes and old Doc Wallace wasn't neither one much for neat handwriting. To figure out the names, I had to study the little tabs real close, working my way down through the stack. There was old and new files all mixed up. I noticed names of folks I knew was dead, along with ones who wasn't. I wondered if Dr. Fellowes ever put anything away. From the size of the stack, I didn't guess so. As I got one family name deciphered, I'd push that file back in the pile and slide out the next one.

I didn't notice how my pushing in and pulling out was making that stack go lopsided, and all at once the whole pile fell right over to the floor.

Dismayed, I tried to scoop the mess up real careful, but the files dripped out loose papers and notes what were stuck in but not fastened down.

"I sure hope he's got a lot of house calls to make today," I murmured to Keely Faye, who was sitting in a playpen Dr. Fellowes found in the clinic when he took it over from old Doc Wallace. Keely Faye jabbered nonsense at me while I spread out the mess of files and papers and tried to sort it all out.

I was partway through when I came across a file titled *Keddrington*, which I saw had notes from when I took Keely Faye in to see the doctor. Curious, I glanced through the other papers in the file, most of which were hooked down with a fastener and appeared to date way back to times when Pa's first wife was alive.

Now that there was an odd thing. I knew for a fact Pa had married his first wife up north somewhere. I never really knew how or where they met, just assumed it was wherever they got married at, 'cause I couldn't figure out why else they'da lived so far away from Pa's ma, who was alive back then. Come to think of it, what was Pa doing up north, anyway? I realized I didn't know one thing about Georgie's ma's family, where she was from or even what her name was. I never thought about it before, how I knew so much about my great-great-great-grandpa and his offspring but never thought to wonder these things about my own pa and his first wife.

Wondering if this file might hold some answers to questions I was ashamed I'd never asked before, I scanned through the different papers, not sure what I might find.

An hour later Dr. Fellowes found me, sitting in that pile of files, staring into space and trying not to cry. When he realized what I was looking at, he stopped dead in his tracks. His hands clenched up in fists, and all the air inside him blew out in a blast.

"What in the world are you doing with my files?" He was angry, very angry as he lunged at me, looking as if he would yank me out of there. When he saw I held the Keddrington file, he froze up tight. I just looked at him, and he looked back, seeing that I knew and it was already too late.

"I knocked them over," I answered steadily. "I knocked them over and they made a mess and I was just trying to put them back together. That's how I came across this." I held the Keddrington file out toward him.

He put his arm down slow, the muscles in his neck working, his jaw tight. When he finally made a sound, it was a whisper. "So you know" was all he said, and I nodded.

Dr. Fellowes sank down in a chair, burying his face in his hands. He sat like that so long I wondered if he'd fell to sleep. But he hadn't. He'd likely not sleep well again for a long time.

"Tell me what it means," I commanded, rising up off the floor. Something was choking me, some emotion I hadn't ever felt before. It made my tongue taste like metal, made my heart pound in my ears. I couldn't breathe, I was so jarred by what was happening. It was a whole new tragedy, so quick upon the heels of Ma's dying and then Pa's being killed by that awful bull. Now I had lost another person, and this time it was Georgie. 'Cause from what Doc Wallace wrote in that there file, I had just learned that Georgie's not my sister. Not a half, not any other fraction. She's not my sister at all. And top of that, she's part Negro.

I never fainted 'fore in my whole life. It was a good thing Dr. Fellowes caught me as I fell.

"Says in the file Georgie's ma was named Lynetta."

It was later, much later, after I woke up and stopped the crying that at first I thought would never stop. Now I was sitting on a stool, the glass of water Dr. Fellowes brung me at my elbow. Keely Faye had fell to sleep in the playpen in the parlor and Dr. Fellowes was sitting next to me. I wasn't sure I wanted to be close to him who had been keeping all these secrets all this time. But I didn't have the energy to squirm away.

"Yes," Dr. Fellowes finally breathed out heavy. "She was. Lynetta Bates, that was her name before she got married."

"Says in the file," I held my voice steady, even though it wanted to shake, "says in the file that Pa met Lynetta up north and fell in love, just after she got widowed."

Like the widder. Like the widder from the shop. Where Georgie was right now.

Dr. Fellowes nodded. "She was married to a white man."

"And Georgie's mama wasn't. White, I mean. She wasn't white?"

Dr. Fellowes shook his head. "Lynetta was half Negro. There's places that it's not against the law, where colored folks and white folks are allowed to mix and even marry. Her husband, fellow by the name of Richard Hewitt, worked at making steel in Pennsylvania. Died in an accident at the factory."

"What kind of accident?"

"An accident, one of those things that happens all the time when people work around machines and molten, boiling steel. I guess . . . " His voice trailed off a bit, then he picked back up the thread of his thought. "Your pa never did believe it was an accident, though, and there was some indication it might not have been."

"Might not have been an accident? You mean that . . . somebody killed him? Wanted him to die bad enough to kill him?"

Dr. Fellowes walked over to the window and sat down on the radiator, facing outside to the town. When he answered his voice was full of hurt.

"Georgie's pa was married to a woman who was part Negro. It was legal up north, not like here, but even being legal, things like that stick in some folks' craws, get them all riled up when it shouldn't. Georgie's father being married to a colored woman apparently got somebody riled enough they—"

"Killed him," I finished it for him.

Dr. Fellowes got up off the radiator and came back to where I was sitting. He sat down beside me, so he could talk to me more quiet than from across the room.

"It was a long time ago, and we're not in possession of the facts. I don't know if killing him was their intention," he said. "Could be things just got too far out of hand." He shook his head. "Whatever the intention, Georgie's father died, left Lynetta a widow, expecting their baby."

The last part came out kind of awkward, like he had to finish saying something he wasn't glad he'd started. Dr. Fellowes shifted his position, kind of squirming, and I felt his elbow brush a little bit against mine.

I moved my arm away, and then scooted myself a few feet over.

Secrets was just like lies, far as I was concerned, and I didn't have much use for any liar.

I had to bust up the silence, though, laying heavy in that room around us. "Why couldn't they just leave well enough alone?" I said. "Lynetta and her husband wasn't hurting anyone, were they? They weren't breaking any law. Why can't people just leave their noses out of where they don't belong?"

Dr. Fellowes was gentleman enough not to mention how it was my nose where it didn't belong that brung us to this place. He just said, "Even when such things are legal, there's always those that take exception." I could tell he was pretending he didn't know I'd moved my arm and my whole self as far away from him as space allowed.

"Hmmph," I said, because I couldn't think of anything else to say. Then I thought of what I wanted to know next. "So Lynetta's husband got killed by white folks? What did that have to do with Pa? How'd he ever come to marry her, anyway?"

"What happened to Lynetta's husband wasn't anything to do with your pa, Mony." Then he paused. "Well, actually, I guess it was. See, Richard Hewitt was a fellow from here in

Torsten. He left Torsten to go up north because he hated things about this place."

"Things? What things?"

"Jim Crow. He hated Jim Crow." The big old clock up on the wall ticked on as Dr. Fellowes added carefully, "Richard Hewitt hated Jim Crow much as your pa did. That's why they went up north together to find work. To get away from here."

Then it sunk in. The name. Hewitt. Pa and a man named Hewitt.

"Richard Hewitt, from here in Torsten? Hewitt?" I spluttered. "Like Mr. Hewitt? From the bank?"

Dr. Fellowes nodded. "Brothers. Not much alike, though. Least, not in how they thought."

"So Pa and Lynetta . . . "

Dr. Fellowes sighed. "Your pa knew Lynetta would have a tough time of it when Richard died, tried to do what he could to help her through it. Helped her pick a spot to bury Richard, kind of put her life back together much as it could be put.

"Anyway, your pa tried to help Lynetta through her hard time, but they could both see there was harder times ahead. There'd be a baby soon, and Lynetta would be a woman all alone, with no husband."

"Didn't take too much for your pa to realize he was in love with her. But it must have taken a lot of courage for him to marry her. And for her to marry him." Dr. Fellowes cleared his throat and kind of shook his head. He seemed like a man what had been off in another place and was trying to find his way back to where he left off.

"Anyway. Your pa and Lynetta got married up there in Pennsylvania. They were planning to go on living there, except Lynetta died when Georgie came." Dr. Fellowes looked down at his hands. "Sometimes that happens," he said, sounding as sorry as if it were his own fault. But it couldn't have been. Dr. Fellowes had stumbled into this long after Georgie come into the world.

"Rather than stay up there where he didn't have any roots or kin, your pa brought the baby and came back here to live and raise her. Nobody ever knew who her mama was. There wasn't anybody here in Torsten who knew about Lynetta, not even Richard Hewitt's brother. Your pa hated what had been done to Richard and Lynetta and couldn't bear the thought of their child facing trouble over her color, especially here in the South. The only soul who knew the facts was old Doc Wallace, and he found out by accident. Seems your pa was troubled by some small discolorations on Georgie's back, so he took her to Doc Wallace. Doc Wallace recognized the spots as a benign condition typical to babies of color. That's when the truth came out, and old Doc Wallace saw the wisdom in keeping the story under wraps. He documented the facts in that file you found, and filled me in when I took over, but he never told another soul."

Georgie's not my sister.

Georgie, with her dark curls and eyes, the way we didn't look at all alike.

Pa, of course, had known.

I remembered that day of the barbershop and the men lying in that pile of busted glass. No wonder Pa had said the things he said and did the things he done.

It was all 'cause of Lynetta and Richard. And their daughter, Georgie.

But no one ever told me.

I didn't want to be mad at Pa for this. But he didn't have no right to keep such things from me. What else had he kept secret? What other things in my life was a lie?

"Mony, you understand that Georgie must not ever know."

I was being so angry at my pa right then, I'd forgot all about Dr. Fellowes.

Till he commanded, "You must not breathe a word of this to Georgie."

Pleading, he was. Commanding and pleading all at the same time. Looking at me with them eyes, begging.

It occurred to me that this weren't all about me. It was about Georgie, too, about Georgie most of all.

"And why not? Don't you think she has a right to know about where she come from?"

His answer was real low. "Georgie wouldn't understand. She wouldn't realize the consequences if this got out."

"What consequences?" I couldn't imagine what the doctor meant.

"If it were known that Georgie is part colored, you can't imagine what might happen. All the people that you think of as your friends . . . the ladies who come into Georgie's shop . . . it would all be over."

"How can you say that?" I hated him, in all his Yankee smugness. Thinking he knew more about this town than those what lived here. "Unlike you, we've lived here all our lives. People know us, me and Georgie. They like Georgie. They like her dresses. . . . "

"Don't you remember Harry Johnson? Those were his friends, Mony. People who'd known him all his life."

I did remember. Them folks had been getting theirselves kept presentable by Harry Johnson since they was all boys. Them folks what threw him through his window. Turned his skin to shreds. Coulda killed him. Maybe wanted to. And he was white.

What would they do to Georgie? My stomach heaved.

"You've seen the little signs up everywhere that say 'Whites Only'?" Dr. Fellowes's voice was gentle as he went on. "They'd be aimed at Georgie. People would shun her. There's places she'd not be allowed to go. Shops. Whole streets. Would you want people spitting on your sister?"

I closed my eyes. "They wouldn't," I insisted, hoping I was right, but not believing it.

"There's more to think about. There's the mortgage on your farm to consider. The mortgage Mr. Hewitt holds. Think of how he was with Harry Johnson. You'd lose your farm, Mony, and you'd lose it to him. People wouldn't come into the dress shop anymore, and Georgie would lose the shop. You have a mortgage now. . . . You'd lose your home."

The room was spinning. But Dr. Fellowes wasn't finished yet.

"People finding out about Georgie would mean the end of your family, too, for sure. Do you think anyone would allow a colored girl to raise two little white girls she wasn't related to? They'd step in, Mony, and you and Georgie and Keely

Faye would not be allowed to be a family anymore. Magnolia Hewitt would have Keely Faye so quick. . . . Can you do that to your sisters?"

It was hard there, teetering on the edge of the world between being a little girl and being a grown-up. It was hard to stay rational when I still had my ma and pa and things was going good. It was hard to stay rational then, but I surely couldn't do it now. Not when things was going so completely crazy.

My present and future life was falling to pieces around me, while other things, long past, was falling into place. The voices of the ladies in our parlor that day, Mrs. Hodges and Mrs. Hedgewick, talking 'bout what Dr. Fellowes did. They didn't have the full story, but they had enough so I could see how it must have happened. It weren't no patriotic fervor Dr. Fellowes had plied Adam with. Dr. Fellowes knew how Torsten folks was thinking and feeling. He figured Adam was cut out of the same bigoted cloth, and saw his opportunity to get Georgie for hisself. He musta told all of this huge secret right to Adam. And Adam, in a fit of rage, had run off and joined the army. To get away from Georgie, 'cause he hated colored folks.

Now suddenly, I knew who I was mad at. It was Dr. Carter Fellowes, talking on and on about keeping this a secret to protect Georgie. When he was the very one who told the only person ever mattered to her. Cost her the man she loved.

"Why couldn't you just let them well enough alone?" I felt like screaming, but my voice came out in a whisper.

"Let who alone, Mony?" Dr. Fellowes looked bewildered.

"Georgie and Adam." I shook my head, my voice rising

again. "You might have just told *her* the truth, instead of telling Adam. All your fine talk of keeping this a secret to protect her . . . didn't you consider Adam might spread it around?"

Dr. Fellowes shook his head, looking a bit riled hisself. "I didn't breathe a word of this to Adam."

"I don't care what you say, every biddy in this town knows that's exactly what you did."

He shook his head, more violent this time. "Mony, I swear to you, I didn't talk to Adam. Not about her ma, not about the war, not about anything."

"Then why else would Adam go off like that?" I was near to wailing now.

He held his hands out, palms up, and shook his head. "I've wondered that myself."

Now I was really confused. "But why, when everybody said you shamed him into going, why didn't you defend yourself? Why didn't you come out and say it was a lie?"

There wasn't any understanding grown-ups, I realized. Specially this particular one.

He scuffed his toe in the floor like digging a hole in the dirt for marbles. Sheepish, that's what he was acting. Caught, and feeling foolish with me there, examining his feelings underneath the microscope of my looking at him.

"Mony, you know how much I care for Georgie. When Adam up and left, all I could think was how folks would talk. I guess . . . " Here he paused, looking off in space. Then he took a deep breath. "I thought Adam must have figured out the truth somehow, and I didn't want folks speculating, wondering why Adam jilted her. I couldn't stand the thought of what might get around, so I invented my own rumor and let that get around instead. I let folks think I shamed him into going. I figured that was safest in the end for Georgie."

"You knew she'd hate you for it."

He nodded. "I figured that she might."

"But you still did it."

"I didn't know what else to do." He looked hopeless and emptied out.

The story spilled, Dr. Fellowes had almost run out of words. Except for one last thing.

"Swear to me you will not tell. Georgie must never find out any of this," he said. "Let her continue to think of herself as a Keddrington. There's no good to come of her learning about her mama, what happened to her father."

My head was spinning as I tried to sort it out. I didn't know what to think, it was all so confusing. Georgie had lost her father to murderers, but didn't even know it. Then she had the innocent bad luck to fall in love with a man who jilted her 'cause of something she didn't have no hand in.

Then I felt bad for Lynetta, widowed by them same murderers, then dying giving birth to a daughter who didn't even know her mama's name. I felt bad for Georgie's father, killed 'cause of his wife's skin color. And then there was my pa, who loved Lynetta but lost her in the end. And finally Dr. Fellowes, who lost the girl he loved by trying to protect her.

But even with all that, I still felt most awful for myself. I had lost my ma and my pa, and now I had lost my sister, and there wasn't anything that could fix that.

Dr. Fellowes was right. Georgie must never know the

smallest bit of this. If Georgie ever found out the truth, she would have nothing keeping her in Torsten. Nothing to keep her here, looking out for us. For me. No reason to stay for two girls who weren't her sisters.

So I promised Dr. Fellowes—Georgie must never hear the truth.

CHAPTER TWELVE

Laying in my bed that night, Georgie softly breathing nearby, I thought about Georgie's dreams of Paris and New York. If she found out we weren't her family after all . . . then what? I peered through the dark toward where Keely Faye was sleeping quietly. Georgie's pa was gone. Georgie's ma was gone. Keely Faye and me didn't have nothing to do with those people. Pa was our pa, and Ma was our ma.

Georgie wasn't our sister.

I sat up straight in the bed, hugging my knees to stop the shaking that overtook them so sudden. If Georgie found out Keely Faye wasn't her sister, what was to keep her from giving the baby over to Magnolia to raise? Keely Faye was worth a thousand dollars to Georgie, a thousand dollars that could get her a long way toward Paris and New York, and studying besides. And if Georgie and Keely Faye were gone, what was to become of me?

No, I could never let Georgie know. I would keep my promise to Dr. Fellowes.

There weren't much moon that night, no light to spill inside the room and fill out the sharp corners of the darkness. I stared into the dark as if there were something there to see. It was like being on a Ferris wheel, getting took up to the sky where everything below me was revealed and there weren't no more secrets from my eyes. Then sweeping back down to earth where the revelations couldn't help me none, and there was only hard ground beneath my feet. Then up again, round and round, remembering the things I'd learned that day, that Georgie had the blood of different people in her veins, not just the blood of other families, but another whole people filling one quarter of her veins. Up and down, round and round, all night I couldn't sleep a wink.

Maybe 'cause I had to keep it to myself, that conversation with the doctor kept eating at my insides.

I wished Dr. Fellowes was mistaken 'bout how people would treat Georgie. For a whole day I tried to believe he was. But the more I thought about the world I was growing into, the more I remembered Harry Johnson and knew such things was fully possible. It's a terrible thing to grow up and find out what people's really made of, how awful they can be to each other for no good reason.

The whole thing was just eating at me so, I needed bad to talk to someone who could help me sort it out. But all I had was Georgie, and I couldn't talk to her.

I went next morning to the shop to work the money books. With all that was a-tussle in my mind, I couldn't get the numbers to work out. Georgie was scurrying about like always, but by noon all I had done was wear a lot of holes in the ledger papers from erasing. I sighed as I put things back in order and tucked the books back on the shelf. Weren't no use in trying to do numbers today.

Georgie came into the back room just as I was fixing to wake Keely Faye from napping in the corner so's I could play with her.

"You go along home, Mony," Georgie said, stopping me from hauling Keely Faye out of her sleep. "She'll be just fine, and I'll bring her with me when it's closing time. That'll give you a little rest."

I guess even with all her scurrying, Georgie could tell something was bothering me real fierce. I couldn't hardly look at her, but I did try to mumble my small thanks.

So there I was, with a whole afternoon off. Took me just a couple seconds to decide what to do with it. Torsten doesn't have a real big library, just a house they filled up with books and a couple reading tables. It was named after a lady who taught school for close to fifty years when there was just a one-room place to teach in. As a tribute to her, there was a sign across the portico that said HELEN RUTH JOSEPHS MEMORIAL LIBRARY. It was only open Monday and Wednesday from noon till two, and Thursdays between six and nine. The books were old, but it was the only library I knew of, so I went there.

I started at one corner, scanning titles, trying to figure what it was I hoped to find. I'd ruled out one whole wall and corner when I swallowed my pride to ask for help. To run the library during its few open hours, the ladies of the town took turns. It was my usual luck to find the library volunteer of the day was our gossipy neighbor, Mrs. Hodges. I remembered like it was yesterday how she and Mrs. Hedgewick was at our house that day, spreading Dr. Fellowes's rumor as if it was their own. The last time I saw her she was sobbing her phony eyes out at Pa's funeral. Since we became orphans, she never once stopped by with a pie or dustrag trying to help us out like good neighbors do.

"Busybody," I mumbled under my breath, then squared

up my shoulders and marched over to the desk where she was writing things on little cards.

"Hello, Mony, dear. And how are you girls getting on?"

Well, Mrs. Hodges, we're starving to death, but we manage to keep it to ourselves. Magnolia Hewitt is tormenting us, and we got us a mortgage on our farm and no hope to pay. Thank you so much for asking.

Out loud, I confined myself to just, "We're doing fine." I wasn't thinking all too clear right then, but I was clear enough to recognize I needed her help more than I needed to mouth off.

"Is there something you are looking for in particular?" she asked, all businesslike.

I didn't want to confide my errand to Mrs. Hodges. Not when her mouth dripped gossip like a busted faucet. I thought fast. "I'm doing a report. For school. On laws."

As soon as I said it, I realized my mistake. Here it was near to August, and there hadn't been no school for months.

"It's extra work," I stammered, trying to think fast. "For history. I . . . what with all the trouble in the spring, I missed a lot of school. So now I have to make it up. That's what I'm doing, making it all up."

I was making it up, all right, and never was too good at lying. But Mrs. Hodges didn't seem to catch on to my fib. She just shook her head. "This isn't a law library, dear." She leaned forward and dropped her voice like she was imparting a big confidence. "Most of our books are just for reading. Like novels. Made-up stories. Not law books."

"Well, don't you have some . . . history books?"

"What type of history?" She folded her hands all prim

and proper, looking at me over her silly little half-spectacles. "American? Classical? World? Modern? Exactly what is it you're looking for?"

I'd just have to blurt it out or forget it.

"I want to look up stuff about the segregation laws."

She blinked, and something about her spectacles distorted what I could see of her eyes. I thought for just one second I was looking at a strange kind of toad woman.

"You're much too young to think on such things." Mrs. Hodges pursed her lips and shook her head. "Perhaps you should choose another subject."

And Georgie and I thought we needed a grown-up in our lives. Hmmph.

I shook my head. "Never mind." I backed away from her, wishing she would blink again so I could see the toad behind the glasses. "It doesn't matter."

She was nodding as my fingers found the doorknob. "Yes, Mony. You're right. All of that kind of thing . . . it doesn't matter. Not to us."

I fled.

As I was walking down the street, I saw the sign. There on the diner it was, wrote with paint on a board. WHITES ONLY. Big as day.

I musta seen it a hundred times before, but that day I stopped in my tracks and studied it. The old paint that made the white background was faded and peeling. I wondered how old the sign was. I wondered how long it had been nailed there.

I pictured someone long ago painting this sign. It wasn't

simply hate that painted signs like this. It was fear as well—fear about not knowing what was ahead.

The thought gave me comfort. I didn't know how to fight hate. But fear is just not knowing.

To fight that, all you need is knowing and teaching.

I needed to talk to someone. Thinking on teaching made me think of Pastor Wilkins and I remembered what Dr. Fellowes said, about doctors and ministers having special privileges to keep confidence.

I didn't really know Pastor Wilkins too well. All I knew of him was from the sermons that he preached on Sundays, calling on all the folks in town to show kindness one to another. I never had the impression folks was listening, but I thought a man so committed to kindness might have feelings touching near my own.

I counted myself lucky the pastor was to home when I knocked. He was a bit surprised to see me in the middle of the week to be sure, but he let me in and led me to his study. I sat where he told me to, in a chair that like to swallow me all up it was so soft and deep. The pastor kind of leaned toward me from his chair cross a little braided rug from where I was perched.

"What brings you here, my child?"

I meant to say it careful, not getting right to what I thought, but kind of hinting round the edges. I'd been thinking over how to say it best the whole way walking there. So there weren't nobody more surprised than me when I blurted out my question, not delicate and polite like I had planned, but just plain blunt.

"Why is there laws that say everything between the

Negroes and the rest of us have to be so separated?"

He got over his surprise pretty quick. Once he got his throat all cleared and his hands laced up tight in his lap, he was able to answer right smooth. "Well, I suppose the answer goes way back in history. Way, way back." He tried to smile and I could see he was stalling. "What ever brings this up, Ramona? What I mean is, things have always been this way. Why is it bothering you so much right now?"

"It's just I never thought about it till . . ." I stopped myself. "I mean, for example, I just found out there is a law that says a person who is even just a little bit Negro can't marry a white person. That's just awful, don't you think?"

If he thought so, he didn't say. All he said was, "It's generally not a subject people think is of much concern to youngsters."

I'd show him youngster. "But don't you think that's just plain mean? Don't you think it isn't right?"

"Well, Mony," he said, real patient-like. "If folks were free to intermarry at will, we'd soon be left with only people neither white nor Negro anymore, but both at once. That is an abomination. It's a misuse of what nature intended."

Some commitment to kindness.

"Don't you think," I began, astounded at my newfound courage, "where it says in the Declaration of Independence people are entitled to the pursuit of happiness it means they are entitled to marry anybody that they please? Don't you think denying that is denying liberty?"

He frowned. "You don't understand, Mony. A child can't."

"You're absolutely right," I nodded my head fierce at him. "I don't understand." I tried to control the shaking in my voice and hands. I felt for a moment like a soldier.

"The law encourages the preserving of racial purity." He was picking his words careful. "It's best for races not to mix, in any way. Not just marriage. It's a tradition that has succeeded for a long time at preventing . . . conflict."

"What conflict?"

"Why, racial conflict. Between the races. The races have to be kept separate. Like dogs have to keep separate from cats. They just aren't the same, and those differences cause conflict."

"But all men are already equal, created equal." Was that really me talking? Being contrary to the pastor? My ears got hot. Ma woulda died from shame seeing what an awful child she raised. 'Cept maybe not. There wasn't much I could do to stand up against these awful laws, but maybe Ma would approve me standing up here and now.

The pastor shifted in his chair. He was getting more uncomfortable. I could see him wishing I'd just go. "They *like* to be separate, Ramona. They *like* having their own schools, their own churches. It's how they maintain their heritage."

It was suddenly clear to me, and I had the answer I'd come looking for. That there weren't no sense to the laws. They wasn't founded on kindness or loving our brothers like the Bible said, nor on our own Constitution. They was made from fear and hate, and a right smart dose of hypocrisy throwed in. I didn't need anyone to explain them to me. It was self-evident what they were. Evil. That's what they were. Plain evil.

I got up and walked out on the pastor without saying good-bye.

It was most four when I left the pastor's house. It would soon be time to start fixing us supper, but there weren't nothing in the house to fix, so I guessed I didn't have to hurry home. Hadn't been no breakfast, either, nor no lunch, 'cept for Keely Faye who got a single boiled egg I saved from yesterday. My stomach was getting used to being empty nearly always, but it still woulda welcomed a plateful of grits or some oatmeal. 'Cept there weren't none, and no promise of any soon. My everyday dress was looser than it ever been before. Me and Georgie, working in the dress shop with all the lovely clothes, looked just like squatters, wearing too-large cast-off clothes from other, well-fed folks.

It probably wasn't good for business, but we couldn't help it none.

I tried to forget my caved-in stomach and my baggy dress. I stomped along the road, but stomping didn't help get out the anger. When I reached the place the creek crossed underneath the road, I scrambled down the bank and kicked my shoes off. Clutching them in one hand, I waded in to take the long way home, splashing up the creek to where it passed the old homestead and crumbling foundation.

My feet was cool, but the rest of me was hot with anger and frustration. I splashed along, still stomping, swatting at mosquitos and not caring that the creek gravel bit into my feet. When I was finally even with the aged trees Phillip Keddrington had loved, I hauled myself out of the creek. I started up the hill toward home, but when I saw the old foundation, all grown over with weeds and blackberry bushes, I had to stop.

Great-great-great-grandpa Phillip would understand why

I was mad. A man found in the road without no pedigree would understand. A man who freed his slaves would know just what I meant. I wished I had a way to talk to him. Or Catalina. She would know what to do. A woman not afraid to sell her petticoat could teach the folks in Torsten a little thing or two.

"The pastor was only saying what he'd always heard. It's not his law," I said out loud.

Except . . .

"They *are* his laws. They belong to all of us. All of us who don't step in to change them."

There hadn't been words spoke here for awful long, but my saying them out loud didn't seem to hurt nothing. The trees stood tall and silent as they'd stood for all those decades since Phillip's house burned down. The stones didn't argue back at me. Nothing here chose to fault my words.

"It's not really the pastor I'm mad at," I explained. "But he was calling them Negroes like they was all one thing, extensions of each other. Like corn is corn and peas are peas. At least us white folks is allowed to be individuals, separate people, not a color."

Not worrying for my dress, I settled myself down atop the sagging stones, my feet hanging in the cellar hole. The scent of catnip come to me, and I reached out to pick a leaf and crush it in my fingers. I held it underneath my nose, breathing in, remembering the catnip tea Mama used to give me when I couldn't sleep. My thoughts was tumbling like the river over rocks beside me, and I sat there a long time, just thinking, feeling what Phillip's stones would say if they could talk.

It was plain to me the fact some of us was one color and some of us was another had split us up so long only because we thought it mattered somehow.

How could it matter, if we was all people?

How could the people making laws not see?

And why did the rest of everybody just sit back and let things be when they were wrong?

Pa hadn't.

I'd been leaning back on my stiff arms, staring at the growed-over cellar hole so long my elbows hurt. When the thought of Pa came in my head, I sat right up straight again.

When Pa didn't like how things were, he said so. In front of people.

In front of people that mattered. Like Mr. Hewitt and his whole rotten bunch.

Like I had with the pastor.

I smiled down at the cellar hole.

Pa did what *felt* right, not what a bad law said *was* right. Like marrying Lynetta. Pa did that because he loved her, didn't matter what the law said.

There was a little wind blowing through all them trees, but it wasn't the wind I heard answering. It was Pa's voice.

"Takes more than saying things, Mony Louise. Takes living them."

Pa had lived them. He stood up to those thugs down at the barbershop, even though he was outnumbered by 'em. He lived what he preached.

Or had he?

It smacked me like a fist: he hadn't lived it, leastways, not

in full. He hadn't said loud and clear Georgie was part colored, had he? He hadn't said he'd married a colored woman.
He kept it a secret, as if it was a shameful thing.

Shouldn't he have proclaimed it didn't matter, in front of
the whole world?

Then there was Phillip. He set his slaves free, but fought
and died on the side that said slavery was right. Wasn't that
wrong, too? If you have a principle, shouldn't you stick to it,
no matter what? If you don't, aren't you as bad as the pastor
and all the Mr. Hewitts of the world, living with one set of
laws for whites and another set for everybody else?

"Oh, Pa," I cried, "you let us all live a big lie. You let us all
live like Georgie was full white, like we was really sisters. You
didn't ever let on to us where she came from. You didn't even
let on to me she ain't related. What's she going to do someday, if she finds out? Don't she have the right to know we're
not family?"

It didn't feel a bit silly, talking to the wind. It felt just right
so I went on.

"There is a line, right smack down the center of the town,
and Georgie can only live on one side of it. Which side, Pa?
Which side should she choose? If she chooses us, isn't she
lying to everyone?"

It was like the answer was there, in the wind. My head
snapped up.

Georgie *is* your sister. Nothing about that is a lie.

I looked at the stones at my feet, and at the land around
me, land that had belonged to the Keddringtons for six
generations. I remembered Pa's other words, said so many
times, "Doesn't matter so much where you come from, so

long as where you wind up is good."

I wasn't Pa's little girl no more. He taught me how to think, and now I was doing it, thinking things out, deciding where to stand, even if it wasn't exactly where he stood. I wasn't even Georgie's little sister anymore, wishing I could be like her, needing her protection. I needed her, for sure, but I could protect myself. What I needed now from Georgie was just her being there.

What would happen to us, if Georgie found out?

CHAPTER THIRTEEN

It was turning into an awful summer. Not just from all that had happened to my family. The weather turned on us, too. It got hotter. Hot and muggy, and I don't know which was worse, the days so warm and wet you could see the steam rise off your arm, or the nights that sat flat, pressing on your chest, suffocating like an old wool blanket that got sweated in. There weren't no escape from the oppressive weather, and there weren't no escape from worrying. Our money was gone, and if I closed my eyes to try to sleep those hot nights, all I saw was that wicked witch Magnolia hovering, waiting for us to fold so she could take our sister. All I thought about was worrying that Georgie might find out what me and Dr. Fellowes knew, and what that would do to our family. If I tried to get away from thinking, hanging my head outside the window in the night, hoping to find some cooler air to breathe, I'd catch the scent of our wilting garden and start worrying about the vegetables, getting all ate up by bugs and bracing to get fried again soon as the sun came up.

I couldn't worry 'bout so many things at once. It wore me down and wore me out until I knew I had to put it all aside or lose my mind.

Luckily, trying to get by on nothing crowded thoughts of Georgie finding out from my mind. In late July the weather got hotter, and I couldn't remember when we'd last had any cash money. Even with the occasional surprise groceries from Dr. Fellowes, we was in a bad way. Georgie's face got longer and tireder every day until she weren't near so pretty anymore. She was looking more and more like me, thin and gray like dishwater. She was working late nights, sewing all those clothes, walking home from the last trolley while it turned to dusk even though we both knowed that was plain foolishness.

Just for a change one Friday, I swung Keely Faye up on my shoulders and we wandered down to the creek. I had to escape from the stuffy house, get far away from the chores and dying garden. It occurred to me Keely Faye had never been down to the creek, and even though she wouldn't understand, I found myself telling her the story.

"This here used to be a house," I told her, pointing at the old stone cellar hole. "A magnificent house, that belonged to your great-great-great-grandpa Phillip. He and his people was rich. They didn't start out that way, mind you. In fact, your great-great-great-grandpa started out with absolutely nothing but his own two hands and lotsa gumption. Hope you inherited some of that gumption, Keely Faye Keddrington, 'cause you're probably going to need it. Us Keddringtons don't seem to have much luck of late."

We was standing on the edge of the cellar hole. Even though it was all overgrowed, you could still see most of the old foundation stones, set in sturdy as you please and still solid even though they was all put there by hand a century ago. In some places stubborn vines and saplings had took hold and set up housekeeping. There was even a growed-up apple tree sprouted out from where the kitchen once had been.

"I wonder who it was dropped the seed that become that tree," I murmured to Keely Faye. "If that used to be the kitchen, I bet there was a lot of seeds could have found their way to nooks and crannies and eventually growed up. I bet your great-great-great-grandpa would get a chuckle now, to see something he left behind was growing. . . . "

I broke off, struck with a new thought. Something he left behind. Whenever Pa talked about the family treasure, I always imagined it sealed up inside a long-forgotten safe-deposit box somewhere in town. Standing there with Keely Faye still on my shoulders, both of us looking at the apple tree that growed up from a seed that found its way into this old foundation, it occurred to me there was a different answer.

Grandpa Phillip *could* have hid his treasure here. In his house.

Stunned, I considered what that might mean. Here we was starving, spite of working and worrying ourselves to the point of collapsing. But if there *was* a treasure, and if it *was* hid here, it would mean deliverance.

I studied that foundation with new eyes. Somewhere in those stones that time had not yet hid, there might be all the answers to our troubles.

Took me only half a second more to make up my mind I would find out.

Georgie looked awful when she came home that next day, which was a Saturday night. I'd spent the morning cleaning the doctor's place, thinking how to best search out the treasure and came up with a plan. I was so excited to get at it I didn't feel like fixing much. There weren't much in the house anyway, so dinner wasn't fancy—I peeled us up two stray potatoes and turned the last bit of corned beef into hash. This was our last food, but I didn't worry like I should have. Things was going to change right soon, I was sure of it.

Georgie didn't even seem to notice what she was eating. She mostly stared at her plate, now and then pushing a bit of food around, once in a while shoveling some in but not ever really tasting what went down. Even in my excitement I felt pretty awful knowing something big was on her mind, not knowing if it was all right to pry.

Finally I had enough. "Georgie, it isn't right for you to mope about. If there's more trouble bothering you, don't you think I have a right to know?"

Georgie put her fork down and looked at me hard, turning something over in her mind, making a decision. Then she looked away from me and sighed. "It's nothing new, and it's nothing more. Just the same trouble we've been in. We're broke, Mony, really broke. We don't have another penny. It's just that simple, but you've known it all along." She sighed. "Just seems worse some days, is all."

It was on the tip of my tongue to tell her about the old foundation. But I didn't. In the pale light there in our kitchen, talk of hidden treasure seemed too much like something little kids would do. I wanted her to think of me as a grown-up partner, and I didn't figure talking about a treasure would convince her she could count on me.

I couldn't hardly believe what came out of her mouth next, though.

"It doesn't make it any easier to know you and that Dr. Carter Fellowes are in cahoots."

I stared at her, my fork halfway to my mouth.

"Cahoots?" I stammered, thinking real fast. "Only reason I go there is to pay off our bill. He's being right generous about it, letting me work off. . . . "

"That's not what I mean." She sighed again. "I know what's been going on, him sneaking around here and suddenly, that night, miraculously, we have food. What did you tell him anyway? That we can't take care of ourselves?" She stood up. "We *can* take care of ourselves, and we will."

I kept my mouth shut. I didn't have no answer handy, but Georgie wasn't interested in anything I mighta said anyway.

"You just tell the good doctor"—she almost spit out the word *doctor*—"that we don't need his charity, thank you very much. We may be broke, but we can still have our dignity. He's not to be bringing anything anymore and that's the end of it."

My, but she was real worked up. All I was thinking was, if I had to choose between dignity and hash, I'd settle for the hash without batting an eye. We'd stretched this last gift till it cried and was gone. Couldn't Georgie's dignity have waited till there was at least one more sackful of food safe in our house?

But I wasn't Georgie. And I wasn't laboring under the misconception Dr. Fellowes had something to do with my first love going off to the war. I wished she knew Dr. Fellowes had nothing to do with that, but I'd made a promise. A self-ish promise, maybe, but one that would keep our family together.

After I cleared the plates and cleaned up the kitchen, I put Keely Faye to bed, then went in to sit with Georgie. She was in the parlor, stabbing a needle in and out of Tandy's dress as fast as she could go. It was hopeless, but I guess she figured if she just sewed faster, maybe she could somehow turn out enough dresses to keep calamity from happening. I watched her a few minutes, and it nearly broke my heart how she was going to keep struggling, working harder, longer, till the end came, till she had to close the shop down and we starved to death.

"Georgie, are we really in so much trouble?"

Georgie had now taken up her sketch pad, furiously drawing and erasing and drawing some more. Still fretting 'bout the dresses for Tandy Mick's wedding. Tandy's ma's dress with all those seed pearls was finally done, but Tandy's dress was turning out to be even harder to do. It had all-over embroidery, more seed pearls, and about a hundred yards of satin train. I knew Georgie was thinking, Tandy's folks was rich, and if these dresses could somehow be finer than anything in the history of the world. . . .

Georgie looked up from her sketching. "It's all right, Mony."

Something was eating at her, more than she was letting on, and I wasn't putting it together. "What's wrong that you're not telling me?"

She shook her head. "It's just . . . you know how tight

things are at the shop. So many people owe us money and they won't be able to pay for weeks yet. There are bills to pay, and with every penny sunk into inventory and extended out on credit, it is very difficult to get through, day to day."

I digested this. "What about the people who owe us money? If they paid up, would there be enough?"

Georgie nodded. "Yes. There would be more than enough. Ever since the widow gave up the shop, things have been looking up as far as business is concerned. We're selling lots of dresses and getting lots of orders. But people won't have money till September, and September is more than a month away."

"Can we go on till then?"

"Goodness sakes, Mony," Georgie looked up. "You're not to worry about this. I can worry plenty for us both." The way she answered told me things was worse than I had imagined. But how?

Don't matter, I took myself firm in hand. Didn't none of it matter. Phillip's treasure would save us.

Georgie tipped her head a little to one side like she was hearing something. "Is that Keely Faye crying? Be an angel and go run and check on her. I'll be along in a few minutes."

I was dismissed, but it didn't hurt my feelings none. I scurried up to our bedroom where Keely Faye was fast asleep, as I knew she would be. I laid out some working clothes and shoes so's I could find them in the dark. I would wait till Georgie was asleep, then slip out and go down to the old foundation and get to work. By this time tomorrow, our troubles would be over.

Georgie didn't notice anything wrong with my hands the next day because I pulled my Sunday gloves on over the raw sores and blisters, gritting my teeth against how it hurt.

It was easy to avoid Dr. Fellowes in church because he sat behind us several pews. My back was stiff and I didn't know how I could get through sitting there, feeling the aches eating at me from the inside out. It was worse than the hunger my breakfast of milk and quarter cup of oatmeal left me with. Without Dr. Fellowes's help, there was never going to be enough to eat. Where our next oatmeal might come from, I didn't trouble to worry about. Just ate it, gulping and grateful as Georgie spooned some into Keely Faye. I never saw if Georgie had a share or not.

Probably not. She'd show Dr. Fellowes just how much she needed him.

Pastor Wilkins droned on and on. Georgie didn't have no inkling how it made me squirm to face Pastor Wilkins cross the pulpit each Sunday. I sighed, shifting my sore body in the chair, thinking back on how I spent the night. I pulled a corner of that foundation in the woods apart even though the dark was too thick to hardly feel through. My lantern didn't help much, only threw sharp shadows here and too much light there as it swung in the nighttime wind. There weren't no moon that night, so I just left the unpiled stones scattered round the cellar hole. I wasn't sure what I was looking for except some kind of telltale marks that might indicate something hid or out of place. Even in the dark like that, I satisfied myself there weren't no markings that I could see from my hands and knees as I crawled over every blessed inch of that old cellar, shining my light much as I could on every square foot. If there were any marks there once, the eighty years since had done them in long ago.

My hands was raw and bleeding when I crawled back into bed just before dawn and slept a little. Then it was time to feed the animals, shovel up their leavings, and get dressed so Georgie, Keely Faye, and I could make the hike to town for church.

Since the church blowed over, meetings was held in the town hall. It didn't feel much like a church, but I didn't think on that too much that day. I curled up my sore fingers in a ball but 'stead of giving me relief, they just hurt worse inside my gloves. I was so busy avoiding people's eyes and looks— from Pastor Wilkins to Mrs. Hodges to Dr. Fellowes—I mostly just studied my lap the whole time. Georgie didn't feel like socializing, neither. We got ourselves past the handshaking at the door and almost trotted home. I had nearly bit my tongue off when the pastor squoze my tore-up hand good-bye, but he didn't know. He didn't say nothing about our meeting and nei-ther did I. I'd never been so glad to get free from church before in all my life. Georgie wanted to get back to her seed pearls, and I had my own errand on my mind.

Soon as we got home I put Keely Faye down for her nap, then took off back down to the creek. I worked in them stones until it was time to milk the cow, then hurried back until it got dark again. Georgie never questioned me. She didn't look so good that night, real tired and full of nerves, and I won-dered how long she was gonna hold out.

It was easier working in the daylight, but by Monday, I was beat. There hadn't been anything to eat since that oatmeal on Sunday. Made it right hard work to lift up a shovel, not to mention all the barn and farm chores. I got up at first light anyway, thinking to get an hour of working in before Georgie would go off to the shop and I'd have full charge of Keely Faye and the farm. I was plumb wore out and weak, but it didn't change what needed to be done. Sighing at the agony ahead, I jumped down among the rocks to start in again.

But I didn't start in. I stood there, feeling weak, surveying the damage I'd done. The rocks were scattered every which way, and I worried I could never get them back into their old places. Not that it mattered, but I was going to feel pretty foolish trying to explain this mess to Georgie when she found out.

And then I realized it *did* matter. Without the foundation to hold it back, the sides of the hole Phillip'd dug with his own two hands would not stand fast. It might take years, but the sharp lines of earth would eventually go slack, the hole would fill in and someday this monument to all our kin would be covered up and gone. Thick vegetation and the apple tree already grew up through where had been the floor, and the fresh, uncovered dirt behind the foundation rocks would itch to give root to more. Without its framework of stones, the cellar hole would soon be gone.

And now, I knew there was no treasure here. I'd been on a fool's errand, wasting precious time and effort to accomplish nothing except destroy what was left of the house my great-great-great-grandpa built. Tears stung at the rawness of my fingers as I brushed my hand across my face.

I didn't have the sense God gave a goat, and everybody knows how little brains He wasted on them. Instead of mucking round in these here rocks, I should have been using what little energy I had left getting real work done.

Defeated, I climbed out of the hole and made my way home.

CHAPTER FOURTEEN

My mind was everyplace else as I worked the doctor's kitchen floor that afternoon with the broom, sweeping but not like I meant it. I was so hungry I could hardly stand. My fingers felt like limp dishrags, my head so light it woulda floated off my shoulders if it weren't stuck on. I saw in the mirror how my eyes was sinking in my skull and the bones in my face was all poking out. I looked like a skeleton. So did my baby sister, plunked down on the floor just watching me, too empty to stir herself much. Keely Faye, who used to be as full of life as a sack of mad cats. Her little eyes today was flat as plates and dull as an old plaster wall.

That morning 'fore I left I'd saw how Georgie looked the worst of all, her eyes ringed with thick shadows that made her look old. And Georgie's skin, which used to be as polished as the sun, was now more like cold oatmeal.

Starving had sucked the freshness out of us. Weren't any of us pretty anymore.

Dr. Fellowes had been quiet since I told him when I came into the clinic not to bring more groceries.

"Did your sister tell you also not to come here anymore?" was his only comment.

"No sir. She didn't mention that."

"Good." He'd handed me the broom. "Then since I am to

provide no more charity, you will have to earn your keep."

Starving like I was, my heart weren't in my sweeping, and it showed. Dr. Fellowes just shook his head as he passed through the kitchen one time. "When are you going to start sweeping, Mony?" he said to me.

"I am sweeping," I grumbled.

"Here," said Dr. Fellowes, sticking a glass of milk into my hand. "Drink this, and give some to the baby, too."

He also made us eat some bread with jam, and it perked me up considerable. I didn't stop to puzzle over if it was betraying Georgie to eat the doctor's food like that. When you ain't had nothing to eat for more than two days, such questions aren't much bother to you and the answer comes real easy.

Next time the doctor passed through the kitchen, I was rolling out a pie crust. The dough was not cooperating, sticking to the rolling pin and tearing itself off in gobs and chunks. My hands were frightful sore, all scratched up and tattered like they was. I was trying to patch the bottom crust back together where it tore when Dr. Fellowes perched hisself on a stool beside the worktable.

That's when he saw my hands was all a mess. He kind of clucked his tongue as he took hold of me, pulling my hands up in the better light so he could study them.

Made me think of Pa when he touched me like that. Made me lonesome and want to cry. Dr. Fellowes put his fingers on my chin and turned my face up toward him.

I hated that worse. Because if I had to look at his face like that I would start to cry, no two ways around it. I kind of jerked my head away and tried to go back to my pie crust.

He stopped me with a hand laid on my shoulder. "What in the world have you done to your hands?"

I couldn't think of anything except the truth. I couldn't be false to Dr. Fellowes no matter how I wanted to. He was being downright kind, and everything else was so discouraging and awful. So I blurted out about the treasure. I waited for him to start laughing. But he didn't. All he said was, "So, you're satisfied the treasure isn't there?"

He got hisself off the stool he was perched on, and walked out of the kitchen into his little clinic. I was thinking he'd left because he didn't want to talk to someone so young and childish, but then he was back and carrying things—scissors, tape and gauze, a bottle of brownish orange tincture of something of other, and a little basin.

"Let's wash you up first." He led me over to the sink where he scrubbed me, not taking much heed of all the stinging. I didn't feel so kindly to him for a bit, 'cause of that. Then he put me on the stool and painted me orange with that medicine. I could only stare and let him do it.

We was partway through the job when he began, "Is anybody really sure there even was a treasure?"

"Pa said . . ." I couldn't remember now exactly what Pa said. "Pa said there coulda been."

"Could have been." He repeated it flatly, like he didn't believe it much.

"Well, there coulda been," I protested. "Even if Pa never said a word, the fact is, lots of folks left treasures hid. And it's real possible some of those treasures ain't been found yet."

"Now why would anybody hide treasure? It just makes no sense."

Why indeed. I didn't want to sputter at him, but it seemed like he was just this side of making fun of me. "Dr. Fellowes, ain't you never heard of pirates? They hid lots of treasure."

"Your great-great-grandpa, or whatever he was, was certainly no pirate. Unless you failed to mention it to me."

"Dr. Fellowes, you are being deliberately unkind." I tried to sound like an adult, not a treasure-hunting child. "Grandpa weren't no pirate. And besides, you're forgetting about the Yankees."

"The Yankees buried treasure here?"

"Of course not. But they was the reason treasure was buried here. Specially General Sherman."

Dr. Fellowes folded his arms across his chest. "I am really lost now, Mony. I think you're going to have to explain all this to me."

"All right, I will." Hmmph. I'd show him I weren't no stupid child. I knew the history well as anybody, having heard it from my pa as well as studied it in school. I could tell this, although I didn't like to talk much about General Sherman. He was the devil hisself, far as I was concerned. It was Sherman burned my great-great-great-grandpa's house, burned it to the ground leaving only a chimney and foundation stones.

But I plowed into my story. "When Sherman came through, there was only women and children left in Georgia, and they was starving. The army was starving, too, but them Yankees knew the folks of the South would never give up the fight, even starving, long as they could stand up. The Yankees figured the only way to end the war was destroy everything that would keep the Confederate army going till the last man.

So Sherman set fire to Atlanta, then marched through Georgia to the sea, destroying everything in his path.

"It 'out-Herods Herod,'" I supplied at this juncture, shuddering, remembering something else I heard once, something from Shakespeare I heard and liked. I paused dramatically.

"But don't you think"—the doctor nodded, defending the Yankee general that singlehanded wiped out a whole state—"it might have been the kindness Sherman thought it was? It hurried the surrender, probably saving what was left of the South from a long, drawn-out death."

"Hmmph," I said again, because I couldn't think of anything else to say. "You sound like a Yankee. I shoulda knowed better than try to explain."

"No need to get huffy, young lady."

"Then forget about Sherman. I got me a floor to sweep." I didn't feel much like respecting my elders right then, not considering how little good they was doing me.

He shook his head. "You've already swept. Go on with your story. Tell me how the treasure figures into all this about people starving."

He seemed so sincere and wanting to understand, I swallowed my miffed pride and went on. "When Sherman came through, people were starving and money was useless as there was nothing left to buy."

He nodded. "So hungry there was people who would have sold their own mother for five minutes alone with a loaf of bread. Or so I've heard."

If Dr. Fellowes suspected on what ground he tread, he would have shut up. I felt a stab in my own guts, and it wasn't hunger this time. It was fear. Terrible fear. If folks woulda sold their own mother back then, what would Georgie do now, almost that desperate and with two little sisters who wasn't really hers?

I shook my head and began again. "Well, there wasn't any money, but there was other things. Them people was rich when the war started. The war took a lot from them, but them that had vision kept some back. Against the future. No matter which side won or lost, the war would be done someday and people would have to have something left to start over with. So some folks thought ahead and hid part of their riches, not letting on to the rest of their kin. They couldn't," I explained. "When things got bad, if folks found out there was any family treasure left, they would have took it and scoured the earth to find one last ear of corn or sack of flour. So folks hid whatever they still had, knowing when the war was finally done, they could dig it up and start over. They knew a body could do a lot after the war, with a little tiny treasure and a lot of gumption."

"Didn't those treasures get dug up, then, when the war was done, to rebuild homes and plant crops?" Dr. Fellowes leaned against the counter. "If your grandpa hid his precious things, aren't they already gone?"

"Grandpa didn't come back, just died without telling anybody what he done. So if there was a treasure, it's still where he put it. I bet," I added, struck by the thought, "there's lotsa family treasures, just like his, hid all over the South 'cause nobody knew to look for them."

Again I had images of gold coins, silver forks, maybe even a pile of jewelry what belonged to someone of our female kin.

"But it isn't there." I shook my head sadly. "There weren't no treasure. So we just got to keep on being poor and out of money. Nothing on the table, nothing in the cupboards."

"And not beholden to the likes of me." Dr. Fellowes smiled. "'Blessed are the poor in spirit, for they shall see God.' That's all I ever hoped for. And the way my fortunes are headed, I should be as well practiced as you in being poor by the time it's my turn to see God."

I was irritated. Dr. Fellowes didn't understand. With only hisself to worry over, he couldn't understand. There was nothing blessed about the way we was living these days. I went back to my pie, laying the top crust on, pinching at the edges, feeling hateful toward rich folks who didn't have to sweep floors to pay their doctor bills, didn't have only dreams of buried treasure to save their livelihood and little sister.

"Mony." He stood up, his voice very kind in spite of that I'd just been acting mean. "Mony, consider your debt paid. Leave this." He took the pie from me. "Go home and look for treasure if you think it's there. If you girls are in such a bad fix, you'll do more good there than here. Go home, sweetheart, and do what you can. For Georgie."

In the quiet, I hesitated. He'd been kind and I could trust him. But I was embarrassed. Dr. Fellowes didn't believe there was no treasure. He just wanted me to make sure for myself, so I could let go the silly notion.

I shook my head. "It was just a foolish daydream, kind of a way to forget."

"Forget your troubles? No, it was a way to believe in the future. Nothing wrong with that, Mony."

I shook my head. Georgie loved us. She wouldn't give up Keely Faye. She wouldn't give up me. Somehow we'd get through this.

Dr. Fellowes put down the pie he'd been holding in his hands. He picked up the stack of papers he was carrying when he come in, then shifted them into his other hand, pretending to glance through them. I could practically hear his brain working.

"You know." He cleared his throat, staring off at the ceiling, like the answer was wrote up there. "Maybe it's *not* so silly. Maybe you really are on to something. If your pa said there was treasure, I'd be willing to stake my life on it, there's treasure."

I perked up. "Do you really think so?"

He nodded, speaking right enthusiastic. "Your pa was a smart man, one of the most intelligent men I knew. So if he said there might be a treasure, you can bet your bottom dollar that there might be."

"Well, I already told you. I tried, and it's not there."

Dr. Fellowes put his hands on my shoulders again, turned me to face him directly. "It's not in the foundation, you mean. That's all you're really sure of. But if it's not there, Mony, where else could it be?"

I blinked. I'd been so certain it would be in the foundation, I hadn't thought about anyplace else.

"Think, Mony." He looked as earnest and excited as I had felt that first night digging in the foundation.

The clock ticked while I thought, coming up empty of ideas. Finally he let out with one. "Is there an old well? Have you considered looking there?"

I shuddered.

He saw my fear. "'Course, you're right. You shouldn't even think about looking in any old well. It's a terrific place to get hurt or trapped. And a well is probably the first place the Yankees would have looked."

All I knew was, I wasn't going down in a well, treasure or no treasure. There was no telling if I could get out again, or what I might find down there that wasn't treasure in any way, shape, or form.

"I don't think it would be hid just buried in the ground someplace." He was thinking out loud as he paced around the kitchen. "Too much chance of it being lost forever that way. You can't exactly dig up the whole farm, can you?"

For Keely Faye I'd dig up the whole state. I thought of her pinched face that used to be so chubby and her eyes that used to be so full of life. Great-great-great-grandpa's farm was hundreds of acres. But I'd dig up every one of them if it meant getting pink back in my sister's cheeks and something besides milk in her tummy on a more regular basis. That's pretty much all she'd had to eat for three days now, was milk from Tess. And the cow was getting downright stingy so there wouldn't be much more of that.

"You know, Mony," Dr. Fellowes broke through my thinking. "Georgia is covered with trees. And lots of them are hollow."

"You think I should go traipsing through the woods peering up the insides of trees?"

Dr. Fellowes shrugged. "Aren't there any old, hollow trees down on your place that's been there for generations? Back before the Civil War? A tree big enough there could be something hid inside?"

Big enough something could be hid inside? I squinted my eyes, thinking, trying to remember.

"Georgie and I played soldiers about a billion times when we was little. We've been inside and outside every hollow tree on the place. We know them better than anything and I tell you, there's no treasure inside any of the trees down there."

But as I was talking, something shook loose in my memory. "Wait. There *is* an old tree, a big old tree that stands all by itself, down on the bank of the creek by the old cellar hole. Pa said Grandpa Phillip always had an uncommon liking for that tree, 'cause it was in such a pretty spot. The tree was already close to a hundred years old back then, but it had took sick once. Pa said Phillip fancied himself something of a tree doctor. He studied that tree, squeezing up inside it as far as he could, to try to figure out what was wrong. He finally cut out part of the tree's very heart, thinking he could cut out the sickness. Then he bricked up the inside and sealed it with cement. It must have helped, because the tree didn't die." I chuckled a little. "Phillip's son and grandson always called that tree The General after Sherman. They said it had a heart of stone, just like Sherman did."

At that, Dr. Fellowes laughed, appreciating the joke. But then he got all serious and leaned down close so he could look straight in my eyes. "Mony, did you ever stop to wonder why he filled that one tree up with bricks and cement?

There's other hollow trees on that farm and he didn't brick up any of them."

I rolled my eyes. "I told you. He loved that tree. It was the biggest tree, right near his house. It was sick. He hoped to save it and he did." Here I was, finally believing there weren't no treasure. I wasn't going to start hoping again.

But Dr. Fellowes had hisself latched onto the thought and wouldn't put it down. "Mony, I don't think your great-great-great-grandpa was stupid, and I bet he wasn't sentimental. If he needed a hiding place, what could be better than pretend he was bricking up a tree only because he loved it? I bet they didn't call that tree The General for nothing. I bet it was a clue, but nobody figured it out. I bet your grandpa hid something in that tree, expecting after the war he'd unbrick it and have it. But he died, Mony, he died before he could tear that tree apart or tell anybody else about the treasure. So it's still there, right where he left it, and if you find it, it's yours to keep. It'll be all yours, all yours and Georgie's and Keely Faye's."

It was too simple. It couldn't be true. But searching the doctor's excited eyes, I could see he believed it completely. I thought of his useless love for Georgie. I could see right down to his heart, could see he wanted to tear out the brick himself with his bare hands and lay the treasure at Georgie's feet.

I looked down at my own sorry hands, better now thanks to his caring, and I wondered how I could get the brick and cement out with them. Dr. Fellowes looked down at them, too. He took them in his hands, cradled them for a few seconds so tender it was like I was his own child. "Mony, I'm sure that treasure is there. But you have to take care of your hands. Take your poor hands home and let them rest and heal a couple days. The treasure won't get up and run away. It isn't going anywhere."

"If they're already a mess—" I started but he cut me off, his voice strict, brooking no nonsense. Just like a pa.

"Mony, you cannot afford infecting them. It's bad enough they've waited this long. No telling what you incubated. Don't make it any worse. As your doctor, I am ordering you to wait at least three days. Then, also as your doctor, I am ordering you to go down to that tree and tear it apart."

It was silly. A grown man, begging me to go look for treasure. But I nodded.

"If those hands get infected, you'll be in the hospital," he reminded me.

I nodded again. I'd be careful. We couldn't afford no more sickness. Soon as I was healed enough, I'd get that treasure, for me, for Keely Faye, and for Georgie. And for Dr. Fellowes.

The thought flushed energy into me. I hurried to finish my cleaning and get set to leave. I still felt foolish. I'd already skipped merrily down one wild goose trail, and I'd wasted a lot of time and energy with that. But Dr. Fellowes looked so sure. Maybe . . .

"If anybody finds out I went treasure hunting not once, but twice, the whole town will split their sides laughing," I told him as I left. "I'll disgrace myself and the Keddrington name besides."

"It will be our secret, cross my heart and hope to die," Dr.

Fellowes assured me solemnly, and I couldn't help but laugh. "Three days. Promise me."

I nodded, then seeing how determined he was, laughed, too. He seemed more relieved than amused.

No two ways around it, I liked this man. No matter what he'd done, or why, I liked him and I wished Georgie could know him like I did, and like him, too.

Three days.

It was torture, waiting. But I had promised, so I waited. My hands improved with the passing of days, but I sure felt things deteriorating in my midsection. We finally got some tomatoes from our garden now it was August, but even that and carrots and a couple early cabbages wasn't filling anybody up. Every single hour was torture, not knowing what I'd find, if there *was* anything to find, and what I'd do if I didn't find nothing. But I'd promised, so I waited.

When it was finally time, I swallowed up my pride and asked Mrs. Hedgewick if she could tend Keely Faye for a few hours, till Georgie could pick her up on her way home from the shop. I couldn't figure how Dr. Fellowes expected me to be able to bust up that cement by myself, so I hauled a bucketload of tools clear down to the creek, hoping something or other would work. The sledgehammer was most promising, but I worked up a sweat in three minutes flat and smashed my feet and shins besides. It took most of an hour to bust up the blob of cement, and another hour working in the cramped space of the tree trunk to pry them bricks apart. It was well after noon when I cleared out the rubble and worked myself inside the tree as far as I dared. By twisting my shoulders and trying not to think about grubs and bugs and other slimy, horrid things, I was able to get most of my torso squoze inside.

There was more room than I woulda thought, and even a little bit of light, slipping in from where woodpeckers drilled out homes. The tree was mostly dead, and I had to wonder how it kept itself standing so long, specially considering the tornado we'd had so recent. I tried not to think about the tornado, feeling with my hands as much of the rotting insides of that tree as I could reach.

The little carved-out shelf was just above my head. I could have missed it in the dark, except for the tiny holes of light poking through the wood. My heart thumped like a machine gun when I found it. Ever so careful, I probed with one hand.

Sure enough, a heavy little box sat up there, waiting for me. In the cramped space, I almost couldn't get it down without dropping it on top of my head. When at last I got it clutched in my fingers, balanced carefully, my shoulders twisting to make room to bring my hands down from above my head, I almost didn't dare take it out of the tree into the light of day.

Actually, I almost couldn't get back out into the light of day. I was close to stuck. It took some doing to get me out of the tree again. The rotted insides was took up with sharp, hard cement crumbles, digging themselves into my back as I squirmed my way out. I felt spots slippery with sweat and a little blood on my back when I finally sat up, freed of the tree, inspecting the heavy wooden box in my hands.

My heart was thumping something fierce, from being both excited and afraid, all at the same time. I tried to still my shaking hands as I studied how to go about opening up this little box. There was a tiny padlock holding a brass clasp shut tight, but a hammer and pliers made quick work of it. My heart still thumping, I lifted the lid to see inside.

I truly stopped breathing when I saw treasure, just like Dr. Fellowes said, just like I'd dreamed about.

There was silver. Forks, knives, teaspoons, tiny picks, and crystal stirring sticks. Twined throughout the cutlery there was a handful of necklaces and gold chains, the heaviest bearing a gold watch, another with a stunning diamond brooch attached. There were other stones—garnets, pearls, and what looked to be sapphires studded onto some of the jewelry. Six or eight loose diamonds in a little muslin bag. And diamond earrings nestled in the bottom, along with a small handful of old, old coins. The coins were for sure real gold. You could tell. The handfuls of silver weighed so much they could not be silver plated. They were silver, real silver, through and through, just like so many rich folks had before the war. All tumbled together, it was, but gleaming and shining as if it weren't 1944 no more, but 1864 all over again.

I lifted a silver fork out of the box, amazed at its heft. The handle was engraved with a fancy letter. Through the generous swirls and loops and whatnots carved into the metal, I could just make out the letter *K*.

Great-great-great-grandpa's silver. His watch, his chains, his coins, his diamonds. I wondered how hastily they'd been tossed into this box to be sealed up in the tree. Maybe at the first sound of Fort Sumter's guns Phillip Thomas Keddrington had selected his best treasures, walked stiffly to the tree, and spent a whole day carefully arranging the bricks and mortar, knowing there might not be time to do it when the need arose.

Either way, I now held them in my hands, spilling out of the plain wooden box with the broken clasp. I didn't have no idea how much all the stuff was worth, but I knew at least this—what I held was more than a fortune, more than I could ever hope, more than even Mr. Hewitt at the bank had ever held in his own hands at once.

I sat there for a time, staring off into the trees but not seeing anything, not hearing anything, not even thinking anything. Just feeling that box, heavy in my hands. I knelt there, lost in time, until a bird up in the leaves set up a fearful racket of scolding and I got yanked back to my own time. My knees were stiff and aching, and the shadows was getting long. It was time to go.

I tucked the box under my shirt, pulling my light jacket up my arms backward to hide the bulge. It wouldn't fool anybody that saw me, but there was likely not to be anybody in these woods. So I hurried home, carrying a fortune hid in my clothes and a future dreamed up in my head.

Magnolia was at our house. When I saw her car, I hurried around to the back door and slipped in, hoping no one heard. Staying out of sight of the parlor, I tiptoed up the stairs to the bedroom, looking for a place to hide the silver so I could march downstairs and tell Magnolia what I thought of her. The treasure would mean we was safe. Magnolia wouldn't get Keely Faye. We could all stay together as a family. I knew Ma wouldn't approve, but for once it didn't matter. I could afford to mouth off to Magnolia now. I shoulda felt guilty even thinking that, but I didn't. Ma wouldn't have approved what Magnolia was doing, neither, so I guessed she'd forgive me for being smart just this once.

I meant to hide the silver under the bedclothes, but there were already things on the bed.

A suitcase.

Clothes.

My clothes. Mine and Keely Faye's.

What was going on? I sank down to the floor, clutching the bedpost. Even clear up here Magnolia's voice carried, and I could hear her words, clear as if it was me sitting in the parlor 'stead of Georgie.

"Just give me the child and it will be over. The bank won't call the loan. You have my word."

"Your word has never been anything I was willing to count on," Georgie was saying coolly.

Call the loan? What did that mean? I tipped my head closer to the door, waiting for more.

"You don't have any choice. You either give me the child or you lose your home. And your shop. Ramona Louise will go to a home somewhere. It's all over for you. You have only a few days left."

Was this what had Georgie worried so, what etched them lines deep in her face and kept it dark like it was covered up with clouds? What made her sew long into the night as fast and furious as she could go? It wasn't just Magnolia wanting Keely Faye. It wasn't just no money while we waited for our neighbors to pay up. The bank was fixing to take away our house right now.

Mr. Hewitt's bank.

"Give me the child today," Magnolia was going on, while I steamed quiet at the stair rail up above. "Give me the child and by tomorrow, your home will be safe, your shop will be safe, and in a few weeks when the crops are in, people will be able to pay you and you can pay off the mortgage and be done with it. I will never trouble you again, and if you want to see the baby once in a while, you may."

I held my breath, praying Georgie hadn't somehow stumbled onto what Dr. Fellowes and I knew, that Keely Faye wasn't kin and had no hold on her. But why the suitcases on the bed?

"Magnolia," Georgie said, and her not calling the woman Mrs. Hewitt showed just what she thought of her, "you are not welcome in this house."

I let out my breath.

"In three days, I will be the owner of this house" was the banker's wife's reply.

"Be that as it may, you are not welcome here today." Georgie's voice was steady. "You'll need to leave at once, or this pleasant visit will turn nasty. You see"—I heard the springs give as Georgie stood up, and I could imagine her leading Magnolia to the door—"you see I intend to discuss all three of your visits to our home with the sheriff, unless you are out of the door by the time I count to five. And to make sure you are, I am going to yell upstairs to Mony, who came in a few minutes ago, and instruct her to bring me Pa's shotgun. Because you are leaving here, one way or another."

"Very well," Magnolia said, a trifle too quickly. I sprung up from my crouching and took pains to step noisily on the old floorboards of the hall to make her think I was coming down, the shotgun resting on my arm.

"I only came here to give you one last chance. Since you don't intend to take it, I shall say good-bye—that is, until three days from now, when I'll take possession of your farm and your shop and all those dresses you have worked so hard on," she said loudly, for my benefit. Then she stomped out the door to her fancy Lincoln car, fired up the engine, and was gone, a fog of dust blowing in the windows at us, all over the curtains and the rugs of the house she intended to have in three days' time.

Me, up there at the top of the long stairs, I finally remembered I should breathe. We was safe, all three of us.

But what about those suitcases? What was Georgie planning?

Georgie met me in the bedroom. When she saw the questions that was in my eyes about the suitcases and the clothes, she stepped forward.

Her voice was small and exhausted. "There's nothing else to do."

"Why are you packing for us?" I was confused, and scared. "What are you planning to do with us? Where are you sending us?"

Georgie looked at me real hard, then spun around on her heel, to yank some things out of the wardrobe. "I'm packing your things because I'm taking you and Keely Faye to an orphanage. It's only temporary. A place for kids whose parents are coming back for them. We may be going to lose the farm in three days, but I don't intend to lose you or Keely Faye."

"Why are we going to lose the farm?"

Georgie sighed, big and long. "A man brought me some papers a few weeks ago. Twenty-seven days ago, to be exact," she said. Her tone was as bad as if we'd lost the war. "The papers said the bank was giving us thirty days."

"Thirty days for what?" I asked, puzzled.

"They're calling in the loan," she answered flat and short.

"Calling in the loan? What does that mean?"

"It means we had exactly thirty days to either pay off the mortgage on this farm or the bank would take it away from us."

Take the farm? No wonder Georgie had been so down lately. "Can they do that?" I finally asked.

She shrugged. "I guess so. They said they would, so I guess they can."

"But it ain't legal. Is . . . is it?" I didn't have no idea what was legal or not. All I knew was, it sounded like they was fixing to steal our farm.

"Who knows what's legal? I'm not a lawyer, Mony, and I sure can't afford one. All I know is the bank says they're going to take the farm and we can't fight them."

"Thirty days? Why thirty days? Can't they wait? Aren't we paying back the money a little bit at a time?"

Georgie sunk onto the bed, and I saw then she was crying. "It's not the bank that doesn't want to wait. Just a few weeks, a few weeks is all we need," she repeated, and I could make out every word, even through the sobs. "A few weeks and we would have been okay. Magnolia knew that. I don't know what she did, she and that no-good husband of hers at the bank, but the end result is three days from now this home won't be ours anymore. The shop will be gone, too. Just a few more weeks and we would have been in the clear. That's why she's making them call in the loan now. She wants Keely Faye. And this is the only way, her last, best chance to get her."

"So why the orphanage?" I demanded to know, bringing

the conversation back. "What right have you got to put us in a orphanage?"

Georgie wiped her tears off. "Even if Magnolia does take away our house and put me out of business, she can't just take Keely Faye. She'll have the state people out here next, telling them about how we have no food, how I'm an unfit guardian, how we have turned into savages who pulled a gun on her and threatened her. Magnolia doesn't intend to lose. I figure she'll be here with the sheriff, the state people, Pastor Wilkins, and whoever else she can get to hustle you and Keely Faye off this place. I figured at least in the orphanage, you and Keely Faye will be well taken care of, while I get a job at the mill. I'll be earning cash money there, and good pay, too, from what they tell me. I'll find a room someplace to stay in, and as soon as I've saved enough to get us a place, I'll come get you."

As Georgie was talking I was getting madder and madder. Not at Magnolia's underhanded dirty tricks. It was Georgie I was boiling over about.

"Why didn't you tell me? Why didn't you let on to what was happening?"

"It's not your problem" was her answer as she folded up a sweater to toss in the suitcase.

"Not my problem?" I couldn't believe my ears. "Magnolia coming in to take my baby sister and my home is not my problem? Losing the shop, which I put lotsa hours into just like you, is not my problem? And now you're putting me into an orphanage? Not my problem?" I was so mad I would have cried, except I couldn't cry and yell at the same time and I wanted more to yell.

"What makes you think you have any right to make all the choices about my life and Keely Faye's? Don't we have no voice in all of this? Don't you think we'd want to stay with you, even if we was homeless, living in a hobo camp beside the railroad tracks? Don't you think we are still a family, even if we got us enemies? Don't you think we should be together in this thing? Don't you think I had a right to know what my future would be?"

All of a sudden I stopped yelling. Here I was asking Georgie to tell me the truth about my future when I was keeping secrets about her myself.

With a whoosh, all the anger went out of me, and I realized Georgie had been planning the only sensible way to keep us together at least down the road.

"I'm sorry, Georgie," I said, kneeling by her side.

She shook her head. "No, you're right. I know how much you've been doing. I should have known you'd want to have a say. I guess . . . I still keep thinking of you as a little girl. But I really know you're not." She looked at me again, her eyes still bleary from so recent crying. "I wanted to protect you, not have you worry. I should have been remembering, without you, we could not have done so well. I could not do what we're doing by myself. You've been with me every single step, shouldering the burden. I should have trusted you."

I let her praise flow through me, knowing things was changed between us forever. Georgie was seeing me as her equal now. It was a good feeling to know she trusted me. Because she should. I knew we were family and family sticks together. Color didn't matter, nor blood neither. Come to think of it, I weren't even related to Phillip, on account of

Jonas, Phillip's own adopted son, my own great-great-grand-father.

I'd never thought this thought before, and it made me chuckle. Because it didn't matter that the same blood didn't run in our veins. Pa had tried to teach us all along that it was love that made a family. And I had enough love for Georgie and Phillip and Ma and Pa and Keely Faye and Catalina to make a family so strong nothing could tear it apart.

So, shouldn't you tell Georgie the truth about herself? said a little voice in my head. Shouldn't you trust her?

I pushed the voice away.

"I'm sorry I yelled at you," I said again, plopping down next to Georgie on the bed.

She put her arm around me. "I know you were scared. I was scared, too. I still am, because this here thing's not over. They will take you anyway, after everything we've done."

"No," I answered, pulling away. "No, they won't. And they won't get the farm, either. Look."

I'd flung the treasure under the pillows before Magnolia left, so now I pulled everything out. Georgie stared. I tried not to smile, seeing her puzzlement.

"What is it?" Georgie asked, after a long time. Then her eyes narrowed. "Where in the world did you get this?"

"I found it. It's Grandpa Phillip Thomas Keddrington's treasure. He hid it in that old hollow tree, The General. Now we can take this up to Atlanta and trade it for money to pay off the mortgage and the shop and there might be enough for you to go study someday besides." I said it all in one breath, the words tumbling all over each other so fast I couldn't hardly hear what I was saying. Georgie didn't hear it either, but her eyes started to shine and then got misty and then she was downright crying again and I was, too. A few minutes ago I was scared to death I was losing my family and my home besides. Now, everything I loved was safe.

We decided Georgie would take the treasure to Atlanta the very next day since we didn't dare chance something happening to it. She crawled up into the attic to find some kind of satchel to carry it all in while I carefully wrapped each piece inside of soft cloths. It was while I was wrapping the silver I noticed something peculiar. All of the pieces carried a matching monogram, the letter *K* for Keddrington, engraved in fancy writing on their handles.

Except for one.

I might have missed it, the difference was so slight. The monogram on this one knife was different. Puzzled, I took the knife over to the window, turning it carefully in the light to figure out what it meant.

There in the light, I could see at once the difference. And I understood what happened. I remembered Dr. Fellowes, how at first he suggested the treasure would be in the well, then changed his mind and suggested the tree, insisted on the tree. Then he made me promise to wait three days, even knowing I was hungry, we were starving, but he relied on the flimsy excuse about my hands.

There in the window, I realized what Carter Fellowes did. This knife I held in my hands was not part of our family's treasure. The knife with the odd monogram had somehow got overlooked by the engraver Dr. Fellowes hired to change his own heirloom silver's crest from an F to a K, so he could fool us into thinking it was ours. How he got it down to the creek and in the tree I'll never know. But he went there, stuck his own treasure up the tree, then cemented it back up, all at night when he thought no one would see.

He made me wait just long enough he'd get it done in time. He'd buried his own treasure in that tree.

For Georgie. For us.

CHAPTER SIXTEEN

It was only two weeks after we sold the silver and jewelry that saved our farm that Magnolia up and packed her things and took off, leaving Mr. Hewitt, his mansion, and his bank behind without so much as a good-bye.

It was nearly September when I overheard Mrs. Hodges telling Mrs. Hedgewick as they pawed through the dresses at Keddrington's how Magnolia should have stayed in town because she would have loved what our store had become. The ladies spent ten minutes comparing a few dresses they thought was Magnolia's style, all the while making it clear how little they had liked her.

"'Course, she won't be needing fancy dresses now that she's not Mrs. Hewitt anymore," Mrs. Hodges snickered. "What is she doing, anyway, up there in Massachusetts?"

"I heard she went to work in an orphanage," Mrs. Hedgewick answered, and my ears perked up at that. "My, how the proud are fallen. She must be so humiliated, surrounded by cast-off children, wiping snotty noses and tying their shoes."

The two ladies laughed. I didn't.

Even after what she tried to do to us, I felt sort of sorry for Magnolia, always wanting something she couldn't have. Hearing what became of her, I was surprised to find myself halfhearted glad for her. Surrounded by children was probably just where she wanted to be.

And she was far away from us, where she wouldn't hurt us anymore. That made me wholehearted glad.

We had plenty of money now. The farm's mortgage was paid off, and Georgie owned the shop free and clear. Keely Faye's cheeks were getting round and pink again and her eyes had spark to them. In a couple weeks folks would be getting their crop money in and coming to us to pay up and we'd have money to expand, 'cording to what the books I was keeping showed. We took the money left from Dr. Fellowes's silver and gold and put it away in the bank where it would draw interest. It was still my secret where the treasure came from 'cause I didn't know what to tell Georgie yet, or Dr. Fellowes. I intended to make sure we paid him back someday, that I knew.

It was coming up to September, and school would start again pretty soon. I hadn't thought about it much all summer, but now it seemed like it would be nice to be able to go back to just being a kid again. Georgie was fixing up the little back room at the shop with toys and things for Keely Faye, and she was fixing on hiring her some help so she'd have more time to play with our little sister during the day when they was both there at the shop. Georgie even said we might be able to hire somebody to come in and help us with the housework so I could concentrate more on studying and she could rest a little when she got home from work.

With everything looking up so nice for us, you'da thought I'd be content. No money troubles anymore, no Magnolia.

But I wasn't content. There was still a question that bothered me. It bothered me both day and night, every time I looked at Georgie.

It was Keely Faye gave me the answer, right there in Dr. Fellowes's kitchen. I hadn't stopped working for Dr. Fellowes. He for sure needed looking after, and I looked forward to seeing him each week. Dr. Fellowes would never replace my pa, but it felt warm and good to be with him, and though the doctor was always busy, he took pains to make time for me. It was the next to the last Saturday before school would start, the next to the last Saturday I would have without worrying over homework or Charlie Jemissee being his usual snotty self. I wouldn't see so much of Dr. Fellowes once school started up. The days I worked for the doctor in his house, it felt like I was wrapped up in a soft old quilt, safe from any kind of storm or awful weather. Like my ma's arms was round me and my pa would be back soon, coming in from chores.

I generally put Keely Faye in Dr. Fellowes's playpen while I worked. But as she growed and took to exploring, she got downright obstinate about being stuck in it. That morning as I tried to work, she set up such a wailing from the playpen I finally gave up.

"Keely Faye, you got yourself a big mouth on you." I tried not to sound too mean, but I was plumb wore out from listening to her screeches. Finally I pulled her out and set her on her feet in the middle of the kitchen.

"I'm going to clean this whole place and make the doctor a nice pie, and you are going to play with these here pans," I told her, arranging all seven of the doctor's frying pans in a circle on the floor. I also gave her a wooden spoon and a couple cans of soup, and I went back to work.

She had herself a fine old time, banging on them pans, then pulling things out of the low cupboards, creeping underneath the table, then leaving the kitchen altogether and climbing halfway up the stairs. I fetched her back and she followed me around while I dusted the parlor and wiped off the windowsills.

While my pie was finally baking, I set to work cleaning up that awful kitchen. Now I was fixing food for him, the doctor was eating more of his meals right here, 'stead of down at the cafe. But folks was always needing him, and from the looks of things, whenever his dinner got interrupted, he never got back to it or remembered to put nothing away. There was a half-eaten roast beef sandwich on the table that already dried to stone, and a bowl atop the icebox with what used to be stew growing a crust of mold. I found a pint of sour milk under Wednesday's newspaper stuck up in a cupboard, and a bowl with old cut-up peaches and cream stashed underneath the Maytag washer.

"What come over him, to make him put his food down here?" I muttered, getting down to my hands and knees to fish those spoiled peaches out into the daylight. "Can't figure what he was thinking when he done it."

Free from her little pen, Keely Faye babbled about the kitchen and smiled. She was so pretty with her little curls and sweet little nonsense voice I had to smile myself. That day she was wearing a little pink romper suit Georgie had made, with puffy sleeves and a little white collar. It bubbled out over her little bottom, exposing her legs, which was chubby again now that we was all eating right. Seeing her so healthy and filled out set me to whistling as I went to work, setting the doctor's kitchen to rights.

I switched on the radio, and hummed along with the bright music as I worked. "Don't sit under the apple tree, with anyone else but me . . . " It was all war stuff, but I didn't think much about the words and what they meant to some sad folks. Didn't even think about Georgie or her soldier. That was all long past, in another lifetime. The cheery music set a bounce in my steps, and the whole morning flew right past.

Keely Faye'd been so content all this while I'd plumb forgot her by the time my pie was done. I opened up the oven door to see it, all browned up nice and bubbling over juice. I pulled on oven mitts to get it out and set it careful, right in the center of the scrubbed up table, leaving the oven door open. That pie was pretty as a summer morning, and I had to step back for a moment and admire it.

I got lost inside a silly daydream, proud of myself and looking at that pie. I was someplace else while Keely Faye, attracted to the open oven door, pulled herself to her feet and got over to it. She laid a hand, her whole forearm, right on that hot, hot door. I was turned away and half across the room, but I heard the awful sizzle, clear and loud before she thought to howl.

Why *had* I left that door open like that? Gasping, sick, I scooped my baby sister up in my arms, not looking at her palm or wanting to see how bad it was. I wasn't thinking clear, just shamed and panicking, wanting to stop the hurt and turn the clock back to where I could do right and shut that door before she could reach for it. I held her hand under the tap in the sink, thinking only to cool the hurt, get the heat out of her palm and fingers and forearm. I didn't dare look to see what I done. My stomach wanted to throw up, I was so full of sick about how stupid I had been.

Her screaming brought Dr. Fellowes running in. I hadn't heard him come back from his house calls, but there he was. He saw the oven open, saw the pie, then saw me sobbing over Keely Faye there at the sink. Didn't take him but an instant to figure it out.

"Let me," he said, easing her, dripping, out of my grip. He hugged her to his chest as he turned over her little hand. I glimpsed the angry, flaming red of her arm, the two or three white blisters already puffing up inside her palm. I turned back to the sink. My stomach knotted up, then heaved, and I hung there folded over the sink, hating myself, hating what I'd been so stupid to let happen.

Dr. Fellowes had a special way about him when it come to doctoring. Even Keely Faye could feel it from him. Watching the pain rage up her arm like to broke my heart all over again. But as he set to work on her, the kindness in his face caught her attention. Her eyes was still spilling tears, her shoulders jerked with sobbing, but her screams was stilled. She watched him as he spread salve on her arm, her fingers, then her palm, and bandaged it all up as gentle as if she was a bubble that he didn't want to break. Then he poured me a glass of ice water, laid me on the couch, sat hisself and her in a big old wing chair, and sang Keely Faye to sleep.

I couldn't look at him, couldn't look at her. I didn't want to go home where Georgie would see what I had done. Dr. Fellowes was studying me, I could feel it. I turned away from him, turned to the wall. I needed to cry, needed to wail out loud, scream that I was sorry. But I couldn't. Not with him there and looking at me.

"Mony."

I squeezed my eyes shut, refusing to turn around. I wouldn't answer him, and he would go away.

"Do you want to hold her now?"

Hold her? How could I? How could I ever look at her again?

"It was an accident, Mony." Dr. Fellowes stood up carefully, took Keely Faye slowly back into the kitchen, where I heard him settle her down in the playpen to sleep. Then he came back in the parlor. I heard him come right over beside the couch where I was laying, heard him kneel down on the floor.

"It's not such a bad burn," he told the backside of my head. "The skin's not charred. For the most part, she's just red and blistered some. I'll need to look at her in a few days. In the meantime, simply keep her bandaged and don't let the blisters break. She'll be fine. And, Mony, it was an accident," he repeated, softly, stroking my hair. "Just an accident."

I wished he wouldn't touch me. All my feelings churned up like that, and he was stroking my hair. It made me miss Ma and Pa so much I had to stop him. I sat up and turned around to face him, and he drew his hand away.

"It was so stupid. I was so stupid."

He shrugged. "Everybody does a stupid thing now and again. It just happened. You mustn't let guilt eat you up. Just learn a lesson from this."

"I've learned a lesson, all right," I said. "From now on, she stays in the playpen. No matter how much she hates it, I won't take the chance of having her out and loose where she can get hurt."

Dr. Fellowes come up off his knees from the floor. Behind him was a little low table. It looked rickety and none too strong, but he sat on it anyway so his face would be level with mine. I cringed, hoping the table would hold him and not crash to the floor.

"The urge to protect is something God gives us caretakers. But He also gives a charge to balance the urge to take care against the need to learn, experience, discover. I know that this has frightened you. You want to build protective walls around Keely Faye, put her safely in a box out of harm's way. But you mustn't. A child this age needs to be free to learn. They fall, they bump, they remember, they start to understand. It's the only way she can become a whole person." He paused, glancing back over his shoulder even though Keely Faye was in the other room and out of sight. Then he went on. "Nobody'd blame you for wanting to protect her. But you can't keep Keely Faye in a playpen all her life."

He was right. But the sight of her little blistered hand would not leave my head. "I just can't bear to think of her ever getting hurt again. So many things can happen. What will it be next time? She's so little."

"You're right," Dr. Fellowes nodded. "She needs to be watched carefully. But she also needs to learn how to take her lumps. She'll soon forget the sting, but carry forever what she's learned. You have to let go her hand, or she'll never learn to steady her feet."

I swallowed hard. His words made sense. Keely Faye didn't belong in a pen. She needed to be free to learn from her mistakes. And so did I.

It was right there, soon as Dr. Fellowes paused, that I stopped thinking about Keely Faye. Dr. Fellowes was telling me something else, and he didn't even know it.

He was telling me about Georgie.

Seemed to me, somebody put Georgie in a box a long time ago, thinking to protect her. It was time for her to get set free.

That was how I decided I was going to tell Georgie what I knew. I didn't like to think ahead, to how she'd feel about it. And, I thought, remembering how upset I was when Georgie had kept the information about the mortgage from me, the hurt of me not telling her sooner.

But I had to tell the doctor first. I was going to break a promise to him, but I hoped if I explained my reasons, he would understand.

Dr. Fellowes had took to driving us home each Saturday when I was finished cleaning up his clinic. "You girls should really get yourselves a car," he'd observed the next week as he dropped me off in our dooryard. "It doesn't make sense for you to be traipsing alone up and down that lane all the time. It's not the safest way to get about."

"We have a car," I said. "We just don't drive it."

"The war's near over," Dr. Fellowes pointed out. "Pretty soon gas won't be scarce or rationed anymore, and all the menfolk will be back. There'll be so many cars on this little road it won't be safe to walk on anymore."

"Hmmph," I said. It was plain Dr. Fellowes spent a lot of

time worrying over Georgie and me. Mostly Georgie, I was pretty sure. But that was okay.

"Dr. Fellowes," I said as we drove past the filling station, headed out for home, "I'm going to tell Georgie where she come from."

"Mony—" he began, but I interrupted.

"I know I promised, and I know you said I shouldn't. But I been thinking, and she needs to know." I wasn't sure how to make him see about Georgie and the box she was in, so I settled on saying just, "Secrets have a way of getting out. You know they do."

"I know," he answered dully, staring straight ahead. "But this one won't. I haven't told anyone. Ever. And neither will you."

I shook my head. "There's too much chance somebody already found out. Just one person needs to find out, and pretty soon, Georgie's the only one in town who doesn't know. She might already be."

Dr. Fellowes cleared his throat, his hands still tight on the steering wheel. "Don't you realize how hard it will be on Georgie if she is told?"

I tried not to let my voice get raised. "What would be hard on her is to find out in the wrong way." I put my hand on Dr. Fellowes's arm. "Dr. Fellowes, I know what you're trying to do. But Georgie don't need protecting. What she needs is to be let out of the box keeping this secret puts her in. It's true, she might get hurt. But the hurt will go away, and just like Keely Faye's fingers, she'll forget the sting." I saw him swallow hard, but he was silent so I pressed on. "It's not protecting her to keep this from her. It's time for her to be set loose.

The way to do that is to tell her the truth. It's her life."

"Oh, Mony." He was turning the car up our lane.

"I'm going to tell her, Dr. Fellowes," I said. I let go his arm, folded my hands in my lap, and looked straight ahead so I wouldn't see the storm brewing on his face. "This has been kept from her long enough. Georgie needs to know and she needs to hear it from me."

He'd slid to a stop in front of our big front porch, and I was jumping out of that car before he pushed the brake. I heard him calling after me, but I didn't care. I was already on the porch, flinging the front door open before he got hisself out from behind the steering wheel.

I don't think it occurred to either of us Georgie would already be to home. She wasn't due till suppertime, but there she was, sitting in the parlor, rocking Keely Faye. I found out later, after all the ruckus died down, Georgie'd closed the shop early and come home, 'cause Keely Faye's blisters and burns, although they was healing up fine, were making her right fussy.

So there she was, there they both was, sitting in the rocking chair when Dr. Fellowes and me busted in the house.

"Shhhhh!" Georgie shielded Keely Faye against her shoulder from our noise, but she weren't quick enough. Keely Faye woke up and took to yowling. Georgie glared at me and the doctor as she stood up.

"There's something I just got to tell you, Georgie," I blurted out.

"Mony, stop!"

I ignored the doctor. Georgie just kept glaring at us, but mostly at him. "And why is he here?" She jerked her head in

Dr. Fellowes's direction, not acknowledging him or saying his name. I could feel how much she loathed him. It hurt me all over again. After all he done.

"He brung me home," I answered.

Georgie's eyebrows went up, but she just said in a kind of steely voice, "Whatever it is you have to say, it will keep until I can put this baby somewhere quiet." With that, she walked past us and up the stairs, still acting downright chilly.

Soon as she was out of sight and earshot, Dr. Fellowes started up his pleadings all over again. I clapped my hands right over my ears so he could see I wasn't listening. "Don't matter what you say; my mind's made up," I said. In fact, I said it three times, not giving him a chance to argue anymore.

When I could see he was stopped talking at me, I dropped my hands from off my ears. I don't know who was more surprised, me or Dr. Fellowes, when I reached up to hug him. I guess I kind of wanted his forgiveness, because I could see he was giving in but was none too happy with me over this.

"Don't you see," I whispered in his ear. "I have to do this. It's right."

"You have no idea what this might do to her."

"I know my sister," I answered. "I think if you knew her like me, you'd know, too." I could tell it pained him to think he didn't know Georgie too well.

"I hope you're right then," he sighed. "Because it doesn't appear that I can talk you out of it."

"Out of what?"

We both turned around quick, surprised she was back already. Now it was too late to turn back, I couldn't find no words.

"Talk her out of what?" Georgie asked again, looking at Dr. Fellowes with a look that would have boiled slabs of ice.

"It was me," I finally said. "It was me that has something to tell you."

"Then let's have it, so this man can get back to whatever we are keeping him from."

"Don't be mad at him, Georgie," I pleaded. "None of this is his fault."

She just folded her arms across her chest and looked at me, waiting.

"The thing is," I started, fumbling until I gathered up myself. "The thing is, there's something I found out that has been kept a secret. I promised Dr. Fellowes here"—at this, I heard him groan behind me, but I just kept talking—"when I found out, I promised him I wouldn't ever tell. But I been thinking about everything, and I know how mad I was at you when you kept secrets from me. I know how mad you'd be someday if you found out accidental, specially since I knew it all along. I guess I figured that it don't show no respect and not much trust to keep this from you any longer. If I found out about it, then you should find out about it. Because it's about you, not me."

Georgie's eyes was getting narrower and narrower, and I realized how much I was running on and saying nothing. "Mony Keddrington, it was early afternoon when you started into this; it's going to be tomorrow 'fore you finish. Can you please get to the point?"

I figured her bad humor was on account of Dr. Fellowes standing there, inside her house and listening to all this which should have been between us. But he was part of this, too, and even though he didn't want me telling, I didn't want him leaving till I was done. I needed him to stand behind me there.

"The point is, Georgie, you and me ain't sisters." It just tumbled out like that. "Officially, that is. You had a different mama."

"I know that, Mony." Georgie sounded exasperated. "You know that I know that."

"Well, fact is, you had a different pa as well. But more than that, your mama was, well, she was half a Negro." There. I'd said it.

Georgie's face didn't change a bit. "Is that what this is all about? Because I already knew that."

"What?"

This came from Dr. Fellowes, not me. I was too stunned to say a thing, just stood there gaping like a fish what had lost its worm.

"Oh, for goodness sakes." Georgie passed a hand across her brow. "Pa told me all about it when I wasn't much more than Keely Faye's age."

"You knew?" I breathed, astonished. "You knew all along?" My head commenced to spinning. "Did Ma know?"

"Of course! Pa told her before they was even married. You don't think he'd keep something like that from her, do you? He figured Ma was entitled to know all, and besides, he couldn't marry anyone that thought it made a difference. Not that it made any difference to Ma. You know how much she loved us all and me, no matter I wasn't her own blood-child."

I stared at Georgie, not caring that my mouth was open. She'd known all along. All I'd went through, worried over . . . and there weren't no need.

"They told me the whole story soon as I was old enough to understand, and old enough to understand it didn't change their love for me. And it never did."

I felt foolish. Georgie'd known all along. She had known

what I was afraid to believe and feel secure about—that we were sisters for always and no one could take that away from us.

Georgie was truly finer than I'd ever given her credit for. But . . .

"How come nobody told *me*?"

This, then, was what was left to hurt. I wasn't protecting anyone by not telling. I wasn't enlightening anyone by telling. I was just finding out nobody wanted me involved in my own family's history.

She shook her head. "Pa told me it was mine to tell or keep."

"Then why didn't you tell me?" I whispered.

Here, maybe for the first time in her life, Georgie looked sheepish. Not looking at me in the eye, she said, "Oh, Mony. How could I?"

I was full angry now, remembering again the day when I found out we was just three days from losing our whole farm. "How could you not? You kept this from me, just like you kept it from me about the bank calling in our loan. Are you keeping other secrets from me, too? Is there other things I ought to know? It's always been secrets with you, hasn't it," I spat out.

"Mony," Georgie was pleading now. "How could I know what you would have felt or what it would have meant to you, finding out I wasn't really your sister? Not even half. And part Negro, too. I was so afraid that if you knew . . . " She kind of glanced up the stairs, toward where she'd just laid Keely Faye back down to sleep. "I almost told you a hundred times . . . but I was so afraid you'd shun me, like folks in town shun the coloreds. Afraid you and Keely Faye when she got bigger wouldn't want me anymore. You would always have each other, and I loved you both so much, I couldn't bear the thought you might turn your back on me and think I was some kind of outsider. That I didn't belong here, with you, on this farm. I was afraid Ma and Pa would have to pick sides, and when they both were gone I was afraid there was no reason left that you would let me stay here if you knew."

I wouldn't let *her* stay? She thought *I'd* turn my back on *her*?

It was kind of funny, except it was so downright sad. Cross purposes. We'd been trying to protect each other, trying to protect ourselves. We hadn't done ourselves no favors by keeping secrets.

Secrets didn't have no place in families. I knew that then. Always waiting to be spilled, always causing trouble till they were. Splitting us apart when we should have been pulling both together. Secrets didn't have no place in this here family. Not no more.

Georgie and I just looked at each other. We didn't say no words because we didn't need to. We was both feeling the shame of secrets, feeling the gladness they was in the open now and wouldn't come between us anymore. Georgie and I was just alike—alike in our love and trust for each other and never wanting to be pulled apart.

After a long minute of us looking at each other, Dr. Fellowes shuffled his feet, reminding us that he was there, which we'd forgotten. Georgie snapped her head to look at him.

"As for you." Georgie looked right at him, full in the face, the first time probably all summer that she stood that near to him. Her voice was a little choked. "I thank you for bringing Mony home, for all you've done. But would you now just get out of our house?"

He looked like he was glad to leave but pained to be dismissed. I knew how much he cared for Georgie, and to have her cold to him just wasn't fair. I decided to step in and put this all to right once and for all. I looked at Dr. Fellowes and I think he knew what I was going to say, because he started shaking his head. But I went on anyway.

"Georgie, there's something else you ought to know. Don't you be mad at Dr. Fellowes. He ain't done nothing bad to you."

"Please, Mony, please don't tell me what to feel toward him," Georgie started, but I interrupted her.

"Fact is, and you know this, if it weren't for Dr. Fellowes, we'd have starved this summer. You found out accidental, but he didn't want you to know. He wasn't doing it to get your attention. He just did it 'cause he cares about you. About all of us."

I figured it was time for Georgie to know the rest—that it weren't Dr. Fellowes shamed Adam into going off to soldiering. I glanced behind me. Dr. Fellowes had sunk down on the bottom of the stairs, shaking his head and looking at the floor. It wasn't fair such a good man could be so hurt and without no reason. I looked up at Georgie, preparing to spill one last thing.

But Georgie beat me.

"It doesn't really matter, Mony, what he did or why. I don't want to talk about it anymore."

"But he didn't do it," I practically stomped my foot to

make her listen. "He didn't send Adam off. It wasn't him."

Dr. Fellowes dropped his head into his hands.

And Georgie?

Just in that quiet voice of hers she said again, "I know that."

The big clock Pa used to wind up every night that I now wound in his place ticked into the sudden silence. I sucked all my breath in and held it there, staring at my sister like she was a brand-new person that I never seen before.

"What do you mean, you know that?"

Georgie sighed. "I guess this is a night we reveal all, isn't it, Mony?"

She paused, as if to get some strength back.

"What I mean is, I knew Dr. Fellowes didn't have a thing to do with Adam going off. Adam went off because he chose to go himself. Funny thing about it was, he didn't go because he was a hero. If anything he was a coward, and that's why he went."

Coward?

"Adam asked me to marry him," Georgie went on, leaning her head against the stair rails one of our grandpas carved. "Before I answered, I told him about my mother. I couldn't marry Adam if he did not know that, could I? So I told him, and he . . . well, he wasn't a gentleman about it."

Georgie's voice said lots more than her words did.

"What'd he do?" I asked.

Georgie looked up at me and smiled the saddest smile I've ever seen. "He spat in my face, Mony."

I ain't never seen such a fierce look as Dr. Carter Fellowes's face was twisted into after Georgie said them words. Good thing Adam Carbee was across the ocean right then. Dr. Fellowes wanted to kill him then for sure, if the Nazis hadn't beat him to it yet.

"He was a coward, Mony, and prejudiced." I don't think Georgie saw the doctor's face. She was looking at me, her soft and awful sad smile still in place. "That's the only reason he went off to fight the war. I think it scared him, how much he hated what I was, and how quickly. So going away was easier than facing me, facing who I was, and what he was. All my feelings that I thought was love drained right out of me then. He wasn't what I thought, nor nothing like it. He was a monster, just like Mr. Hewitt, Mr. Taswell, all the others that day at the barbershop. He was a monster and I never knew till then."

Dr. Fellowes's mouth was dropped open big as mine was. We both stared at my sister.

"Then why . . . ?" I couldn't form a question, couldn't think of anything except what in tarnation was going on.

"Then why am I so angry? At the doctor?"

I nodded. If that was not the reason she was mad at Dr. Fellowes, what ever was?

From off to the side, I noticed Dr. Fellowes had stood up.

"Do you remember how upset you used to be when Pa didn't let you drive the tractor?"

I nodded. It used to make me so mad I could spit. But what in the dickens did that have to do with Dr. Fellowes?

"Now, what if Pa spread rumors round he didn't let you drive the tractor 'cause you couldn't figure out how? Wouldn't you be mad he didn't let you learn before he took it on himself to judge you?"

"What's driving a tractor got to do with—"

Georgie talked right over me.

"When Adam took off, I was glad. I wanted folks to know the reason. Wanted folks to see how foolish all this was. I wanted to be proud of who I was and who my ma was, wanted people to see it didn't make no difference. I could have faced them all, like Pa did at the barbershop. I wanted to. I was ready to, finally, after what Adam did."

Georgie looked square at Dr. Fellowes for the first time all afternoon.

"But you didn't let me. You stepped in with a made-up lie. You stole my chance. I know you thought you were doing me a favor." Georgie was trying to hide the faintest quiver in her voice when she added, "The truth is, there is no shame in being dropped by a coward like Adam Carbee. But you . . . You took my chance to face the world away. You forced me to hide behind a lie because I couldn't set it straight again without making known who told the lie. You're a fine man, Dr. Carter Fellowes, don't think I don't know that. And you're the doctor here, and folks have to trust you if you're to do them any good. I couldn't expose you for a liar. Nobody trusts a lying doctor. This town needs you and I couldn't rob them of you by telling them you'd lied. Oh, it was all so complicated, and the whole thing so foolish anyway!

"So there I was, forced to hide behind you, forced to keep it in, forced to let Adam be the hero, cheated of the perfect chance to stop living a lie. It all seems so foolish now. But can you see the mess you made of things?"

Now all her feelings was said out, it was like Georgie's anger at him had been a balloon. A balloon that all the air was gone from now and didn't have no purpose anymore. If there'd not been no secrets, if Georgie'd had a chance to say all this to him before . . . how different this whole summer might have been.

Dr. Fellowes didn't see her soften. He wasn't looking at her when he shook his head. "I didn't know what else to do," he moaned, not daring to look at her eyes. "I only wanted to protect you. I didn't think this place was ready for the truth."

"No place is ever ready for a lie, Dr. Fellowes. Isn't letting the truth come out on its own kinder in the end? You have to let people make their own life's choices." She swallowed hard, and I could see how much his suffering had grown now he knew his mistake.

Georgie was going on, her voice more soft than ever. It was her apology and her forgiving. "No more secrets, Dr. Carter Fellowes. You're a right fine doctor, able to heal people's ills and fix their broken bones. But you can't fix everything, specially not with lies, and you shouldn't try. Folks have to fight for what they believe is right, not hide behind falsehoods."

There was tears beginning in her eyes, and Georgie wasn't one to let so much of herself show. She turned and marched herself right up the stairs, and I heard our bedroom door close softly. I could almost see her up there, standing still in the center of the room, squeezing her eyes shut to get the tears all out, all at once, then never let them bother her again.

Georgie was free. Not locked up by no more secrets. She was free.

And so was I.

And so was Dr. Fellowes.

The clock ticked a long time in the silent house as we all three digested what had come over us. I finally looked at Dr. Fellowes. When he felt my eyes on him, he stood up, picked up his hat what he'd let drop from his fingers to the floor, and put it on.

"I'd best be off," he said, fixing that hat up on his head. I didn't have no words left in me right that minute, so I just watched him open our big front door and close it quietly behind him.

And he was gone.

I felt so bad for Dr. Fellowes, I walked into town on Monday. When I showed up at his door, the clinic was closed. I knocked and pounded on the door till he finally opened it for me. Surprised, I saw he wasn't dressed in his doctoring clothes. 'Stead of the threadbare jacket and white shirt he'd worn every day of his doctoring life, now he was wearing a regular plain checkered shirt and pants, like everybody else wore.

When I went in his place, I had another shock. Every knickknack, scrap of clothes, all them frying pans was gone. Everything.

"Where's all your things?" I asked, looking around the empty rooms he lived in.

"Sent back home," he answered.

"Home?"

"Up north. My parents' house. I thought it best to send it back, since I don't know where I'll wind up after the war."

"After the war?" I knew I was sounding like a dumb parrot, but he wasn't making sense.

"I've enlisted," Dr. Fellowes told me, and I was getting orphaned all over again.

"Enlisted? In the army or something?" I protested, feeble, feeling weak. "But you're a doctor! You can't be a soldier."

"I won't be a soldier. I'll be a doctor. I can't think where they'd need doctors more." He smiled down at me.

"Just like that? You're going off and leaving us?"

"Yes," he replied, "I'm going off."

"But why?" I cried. Dr. Fellowes couldn't go away. He couldn't.

The doctor sighed. "I can't do this anymore. I can't stay here. You're too young to know, Mony, but take my word for it. It's too awful to be so near to someone that . . . doesn't love you back and there is no hope. . . . "

I gulped. Was Carter Fellowes going to cry? He sounded like it. But he gathered hisself together, all composed, and went on talking.

"It's more than that, though, Mony. I have so much to learn. Georgie was right to be angry with me. There I was, thinking how much I loved her, the whole time I was trying to run her life for her. 'Stead of having faith in her, I was afraid for her and trying to smooth out the path I chose for her to walk. That's not what you do for the people that you love." He shook his head. "You don't nail them down and make them be what you want them to be. You let them go, let them choose their own path. That's what parents do. That's what a man who truly loves a woman should do." He cleared his throat, then put his hand on my shoulder. "Listen to me run on. The truth of the matter is, of all the things I've thought about this summer, most of all is this—my country needs me. It truly does. And I need to go. I've known it, I've put it off, but now's the time at last."

"The war's near to over, least, that's what they say," I argued. "That's what you yourself told me, remember?"

"Near to, but not over yet." He shook his head. "There's still a terrible need over there for doctors. And it's not just the soldiers. The regular people over there, in towns like this one, but towns tore up by war. They need so much help, and it's help I can give."

Now it was my turn to struggle not to cry. "But what about us folks here to home? We still need doctors, the army can't send 'em all over there to help those people when we're still falling ill round here."

He shook his head, a smile still hinting at the corners of his mouth. "Do you think I'd go off and leave Torsten high and dry like that? No, there'll be a new doctor here next week before I leave. Dr. Westmore. From Atlanta. A right fine doctor."

I didn't like any of what was happening. All I knew was, if Dr. Fellowes went away, we'd really be alone. He was our friend.

"Mony." Dr. Fellowes leaned down toward me, his hand on my shoulder. "Mony, it's time for me to go do my part. Now I'm a full-fledged doctor and have some experience under my belt, it makes me ashamed to see these younger fellows going off, not batting an eye. I want to do my part, too. Oh, I know what they say, somebody's got to stay home and keep the country afloat, and even that helps the war effort. But for me, it just doesn't feel right anymore. I'm still young, I'm healthy. I don't have a family to leave behind, like so many of the soldiers do. I belong over there, with them, helping win this war so everybody can come home."

"Even Adam Carbee?" Not till now had I realized the depth of how I hated Adam Carbee. It was wicked and bad, but I didn't want him to ever come home.

Ever.

He nodded. "Even Adam."

"But—"

"But nothing," he interrupted, like it was final. "Dr. Westmore is coming down to take things over here. He'll step in, just for a time, while I go help patch up the world's wounds, maybe see the end of this war and help some people worse off than we are get back on their feet again."

"So you will be coming back? Here?"

Dr. Fellowes looked away from me for a moment. "I don't know," he said. "We'll see what happens."

He stood up and got busy at his desk again, like now the conversation was over and he could go on like nothing was wrong.

But everything was wrong.

"What about us?" I repeated, desperate. I couldn't let this happen. "We need you, Georgie and Keely Faye and I need you," I pleaded. "You're the only real friend we've got."

"You don't need me," he shook his head, smiling. "You've got each other." He laughed a little. "I expect by the time the war is over, you and Georgie will have the best and biggest dress shop in the whole South. I expect soon as they can, the girls over there in Paris and Rome and London will be fighting to get their hands on a Keddrington creation. It won't be too long before the whole world knows Georgie's name, and yours along with it. No, you don't need me," he repeated, finishing up. "You girls have each other."

I opened my mouth to tell him I knew about the silver, that I knew what he'd done for us. But I closed it, realizing if I let on what I knew, he might say, "She must never know." He'd make me promise not to tell. But if I didn't have to promise, I'd be free to tell Georgie what he did. And someday, when he came back from the war . . .

If he came back.

I was overcome with sudden fright. It was a war he was going to after all, and a terrible one. I closed my eyes, trying not to see all the pictures in my head of what might happen to him.

I couldn't stop him going. But I could ask him to promise something. "You will come back," I commanded him, worried. "Promise me. Promise me you will."

"That's a promise only God can make."

"You *must* come back."

"I can promise to try," he told me. It was all he could do, and I felt a little better.

If I'd had a brother, I would have wanted him to be Dr. Fellowes. Now he was leaving me this promise, and it was a good promise. I knew that he would try, and I could hold onto that as long as it took.

"What's wrong, Mony? You look as if you've been crying for seven hours." Georgie was bustling around the shop when I came in after seeing Dr. Fellowes. "Keely Faye's in the back there, looking at some books. I hope she's not tearing them up. Maybe you can sing her to sleep while you do the accounts." She paused in her chatter, frowning at me. "Good heavens, you look so sad. What is wrong?"

"He's gone," I murmured, feeling how immense those words were to us. "Dr. Fellowes. He's gone to be a doctor in the war."

Georgie studied my face, not knowing what she could say. Her voice was soft as petals when she asked me, "Did he mean so much to you?"

"Yes." How I wished I could tell her about Dr. Fellowes, the Dr. Fellowes that I knew. "I wish you knew what he was really like," I finally said, and it was the most true thing I ever told her.

Georgie shook her head. "I'm grateful to him, for being a friend to you. And grateful to him, for trying to help us. But . . . I can't forget what he did. I just can't. I know it isn't very Christian of me, but it's going to take a while to put all that behind me, stop thinking on what he did, what it did to me."

"You don't know what he's done," I argued.

"Mony, you can't ever understand."

"No, it's you who doesn't understand." Remember, I never promised about the knife. I didn't say I wouldn't tell. There wouldn't be no more secrets around here. She had to know. It was only right.

We kept the shop's books in a big locked drawer there in the back room. I'd hid the silver knife in there, since it was the safest place I knew, tucked inside an old ledger the widder Baxter used to sort of keep. We never looked at that old ledger, since the widder's imprecise old numbers didn't have a thing to do with now. I yanked the ledger out from the depths of the drawer and flipped through it till I found the knife. I thrust the knife out toward Georgie. "Look. Look at this."

"Mony," Georgie said, startled. "You kept this? Why?"

"For you to see. Look at the handle."

"Mony . . . "

"Look at it!" I almost screamed the words at her. She *had* to understand.

So Georgie looked. She held the knife with both hands, her eyes bewildered as she studied it. She turned it over, then back again. It caught the light, flashing sparks between us. That was when she saw the engraving. The small, delicate letter *F*, the single tell-tale letter that hadn't matched the others. For a long, long moment she gaped, disbelief freezing her eyeballs in a stare. Then, so slowly, she lifted her whole face to mine. She was seeing me full and clear when her fingers let go the knife and it clattered to our feet.

"I kept it back, to show you. Except for this mistake, we'd have never known what he did."

"It was Dr. Fellowes's treasure that saved the farm?" Georgie's voice came from miles away.

"And Keely Faye. And us, all of us. Dr. Fellowes's treasure saved all of us."

"How can you say that?" she challenged, still reeling in confusion. "You know I never would have let anything happen to us."

"We were going to an orphanage, we were going to be split up. Temporary or not, without his treasure, we would have lost our farm and been split up and who knows what might have happened."

"I would have sold my soul to keep us all together. You know that," she said.

I did know that. But because of Dr. Fellowes, she didn't have to do no such thing. Dr. Fellowes saved our family because he loved Georgie. And he didn't ask for nothing in return.

Loving people was a powerful thing. It could make you do stuff that you never knew you could. Stuff that didn't make no sense but still was right.

Long as you didn't put the folks you loved in boxes, such a thing could help you move the earth, should you ever have the need.

I shook my head, violently now, not caring I was throwing tears in splatters around me. "Dr. Fellowes is the finest man there is, next to Pa."

I wished I could tell her how much Dr. Fellowes loved her. But I didn't. Some things only belong to one person to say.

"Carter Fellowes . . . " Georgie began, as if she was turning it all over in her mind. Her voice got soft. "I'm not as awful as all that, Mony. I know he thought he was protecting me. In his own misguided way, I know he was only trying to do what he thought was right."

Putting her in a box . . . because he couldn't stand to have her hurt.

"And the silver," I added. "Don't forget the silver."

"I will never forget the silver," she told me, and I believed her.

"What he was willing to give up for us, for you, the hard things he did to help us. It's just like Pa. Like what Pa did."

"Pa wouldn't have tried to protect me like that, Mony. He always made me stand on my own two feet."

I sighed.

"But he's as fine as a man can be who's not Pa," she added.

It was a start.

It was strange to think of Georgie now as something more than what I always thought she was. Strange, but good. Every time I saw colored people now, I found myself looking at them different. I wondered if somehow, because of Georgie, I could claim a kinship with them, too.

Lots of things weren't right in our town. And Georgie and I spent many an evening discussing how we fit in. The dividing line ate at us in a big way. One night, Georgie summed it up.

"It isn't fair. I went to a white folks' school. I can sit wherever I want on a bus or the trolley. I can buy my lunch at a whites-only place. And when I die, my picture will be in the front part of the newspaper, not the back where the colored folks are. It isn't right. It isn't fair."

"It isn't right, Georgie, that's for sure." I thought of Pa. And pictured me and Georgie, standing brave and right like Pa did. "But we can change the law, Georgie. You and me will change the law so it's fair, not just for you but for everybody."

"Just you and me are going to change the world? Just like that?"

"Not just us alone, but we can do a little part of it. People's ideas can change, at least, that's what Pa thought. He stepped up when there was a chance to show them just how wrong they was. Enough times they see they're wrong, they'll someday want to set things right."

I remembered the day Pa and I went to town. Pa said we

should fight against what isn't right. Georgie was thinking about that now, how to fight the prejudice and hate, the bad laws and bad ideas. It was 1944, and even though so many soldiers went overseas to fight those things, not many people dared yet to fight those things at home.

But Georgie would. I could see it in her eyes and in her shoulders, the way she straightened them when she remembered Pa. I know Georgie, and she'll do it all right. And Keely Faye and I will be right there too.

With our sister.

Changing the world, one barbershop at a time.

E P I L O G U E

I couldn't leave Phillip Thomas Keddrington's rock foundation all tore apart like that. It wasn't right. So soon as I could, I went back with Pa's thick leather gloves on my hands for protection. I jumped down in that hole and set to work. I didn't aim to do no slapdash job, neither. My ancestors laid them rocks in square and careful, and it was those rocks held up the house so long, till Sherman burnt it down thinking he was helping save the South.

That's when I found the little wooden box. It was tucked down deep inside that foundation. It looked like the rocks was chipped away in back, then replaced over top the space the box rested in. If anybody'd gone down in that cellar looking for something hid, they wouldn'ta noticed anything wrong with the way the rocks looked, at least, not from the front.

Still, how could I have missed it when I took that wall apart? I studied the little box nestled in there. If I'd not been in such a frantic hurry, if I'd had better light, I might have seen it the first time.

"So there really was a treasure," I breathed as I gently extricated the little box from the place it sat hid all during the last century. I held it in my hands a few minutes, imagining my great-great-great-grandpa carving out this hole and tucking his most guarded treasure into it. I wondered how he felt as he set it in its place, then took one last look around before going off to the war. The moment felt precious, and I thought if I looked over my shoulder, I would see him smiling at me, glad at last his treasure was found and in the hands of his family.

I held my breath as I lifted the lid. Inside, tarnished with all the years and loneliness, lay a picture in a silver frame. It wasn't a paper photograph. It was a picture etched right into glass. When I saw how fragile it must be, my fingers shook and I had to sit down, fearful I might drop it, shattering forever the image it carried.

No one had to tell me the woman etched there on the glass in my hand was Catalina Hortense Simons. The boy of perhaps two years old she held on her lap was Phillip, more than a year after she found him in the road. The man beside them, looking more handsome than even Dr. Fellowes or my pa, was Thomas Keddrington, straight to Marietta from Scotland and descended from royalty. I looked at them, feeling tears fall on my knees as I drank in those faces with my eyes. They looked back at me, and with a shiver I knew somehow they were really seeing me there, knowing that I knew them and loved them.

Underneath the picture was tucked a couple books. Even protected as they'd been, the eighty years had left their mark, and I was afraid to lift the covers, afraid the bindings would crack in pieces, the pages dissolve into flakes. Ever so carefully, I turned the books over, gently pulling up the covers just a bit to peek inside. The book on top was Thomas Keddrington's family Bible. As the old-time prophets did, Thomas had inscribed his fathers onto these pages, a long, unbroken line of begatting, fathers and wives, children, ancestors, descendants. The second book was Phillip's journal, in which he told his story, beginning when his mother found him in the road.

"God puts you where he wants you," my pa had always said.

"But I put myself where I want to go," I used to argue, not wanting to believe him, that so much was up to God.

"Then you better make sure you're putting yourself where God wants you to be" was Pa's reply.

That's how Phillip Thomas Keddrington wound up in that road. That's how I wound up here today, with Georgie as my sister and Dr. Fellowes as my friend.

And that's how I came to know, really know what Pa had been trying to tell us all along. Our family's treasure wasn't money. It was a different kind of riches.

It was our history.

It was ourselves.